Kids lov~~e~~
Choose Your O~~wn Adventure~~

CHOOSE YOUR OWN ADVENTURE®

MURDER AT THE OLD WILLOW BOARDING SCHOOL

BY JESSIKA FLECK

ILLUSTRATED BY GABHOR UTOMO
COVER ILLUSTRATED BY BRIAN ANDERSON

CHOOSECO
WAITSFIELD, VERMONT

Book design: Stacey Boyd, Big Eyedea Visual Design
Book layout: Jamie Proctor-Brassard, Letter10 Creative

For information regarding permission, write to:

CHOOSECO®
P.O. Box 46
Waitsfield, Vermont 05673
www.cyoa.com

Publisher's Cataloging-in-Publication Data
Names: Fleck, Jessika, author. | Utomo, Gabhor, illustrator. | Anderson, Brian, cover
    illustrator.
Title: Murder at the Old Willow Boarding School / by Jessika Fleck ; illustrated by
    Gabhor Utomo ; cover illustrated by Brian Anderson.
Description: Waitsfield, VT : Chooseco, 2023. | Includes 44 b&w illustrations. |
    Series: Choose your own adventure. | Audience: Ages 9-12. | Summary: In this in-
    teractive adventure, you need to solve a murder—your own! You are a student at
    the Old Willow Boarding School for gifted children; you wake up one day to find
    you've been murdered. Now a ghost, you have to learn how to communicate with
    others and solve this crime.
Identifiers: ISBN 9781954232167 (softcover)
Subjects: LCSH: Boarding schools -- Juvenile fiction. | Ghost stories -- Juvenile
    fiction. | Murder investigation -- Juvenile fiction. | LCGFT: Detective and
    mystery fiction. | Ghost stories. | Plot-your-own stories. | BISAC: JUVENILE FIC-
    TION / Ghost Stories. | JUVENILE FICTION / Interactive Adventures. | JUVENILE
    FICTION / Mysteries & Detective Stories.
Classification: LCC PZ7.1 F54 2023 | DCC [Fic]--dc22

Printed in Canada

10 9 8 7 6 5 4 3 2 1

Choose Your Own Adventure supports the First Amendment
and celebrates the right to read.

For Mom and Dad . . .
Thank you for always encouraging
me to take adventures!

BEWARE and WARNING!

This book is different from other books.

You and YOU ALONE are in charge of what happens in this story.

There are dangers, choices, adventures, and consequences. YOU must use all of your numerous talents and much of your enormous intelligence. The wrong decision could end in disaster—even death. But don't despair. At any time, YOU can go back and make another choice, alter the path of your story, and change its result.

YOU are a student named Pearl at the Old Willow Boarding School for Gifted Children. After waking up from a strange dream, you go to breakfast with your friends and feel oddly alone. No one looks at you and no one is answering your questions. It's not until you hear a scream and rush to the library to find the sight of your lifeless body that you realize YOU ARE DEAD. Now, as a ghost, you need to solve the mystery of your own murder—but who can you trust? And can you figure out who is behind this crime before the killer strikes again?

Lucy (she/her)

Magnetism

Elwyn (he/him)

*Time travels,
your best friend*

Constance (she/her)

*Communicates with
inanimate objects, your
mortal enemy*

POSSIBLE

Sal (they/them)

*Climbs and balances at
exceptional heights*

Miss Loveland (she/her)

The English Teacher

Jack (he/him)

Speaks in foreign languages, picks locks, convinces others to do his bidding, predicts weather, contorts his body into small spaces

Saelor (she/her)

Controls insects

SUSPECTS

Sawyer (he/him)

Expert knife thrower and archer

The Headmistress (she/her)

Mr. Fitzherbert (he/him)

Headmistress's Assistant

Pearl/YOU (she/her)

Telekinesis

There's Been a Murder

You're falling. Fast.

The night sky and the stone turrets of the Old Willow Boarding School for Gifted Children grow farther and farther away as you plummet toward the unforgiving earth. You flip over midair, and your view is replaced with rapidly approaching grounds—specifically the hedge maze. Its spiked iron fence will not make for a pleasant landing. It's not going to be pretty.

You have no idea how you got here. No matter.

Sharp metal approaches.

In your mind you can see it tearing flesh and cracking bone in the most horrific fashion. It's mere feet away. Inevitable. Then . . .

You awaken.

You sputter and cough, sit up to catch your breath, and work to slow your racing heart. This reality is nearly as curious as your dream: you're not in your bed as you should be, but instead are on the floor of the main library. Books line the walls as far as your sight can reach. It's completely dark save the moonlight seeping in through the windows and the flicker of the candle sconces flanking the fireplace. Their glow casts grotesque shadows over the already creepy portrait of the school's founder. His quoted words, "Each child is a treasure trove of magic—some treasures need only be tamed," are etched into the ornate gold frame.

The antique grandfather clock strikes 1:00 AM.

The mystery of how in the world you ended up here comes second to the dread of getting caught by the Headmistress or her sniveling assistant for being out of the dorms after lights out.

You quickly sneak straight up to your room, climb into bed fully dressed, and fall right back to sleep.

Turn to page 3.

Loud clanging tears you from dreamless rest. It's the final breakfast bell and you can tell by the aggressive ringing that Cook Bonnie is impatient this morning.

Luckily for you, you slept in your uniform. You jump out of bed and rush after the throng of students piling downstairs. You spot Lucy not far ahead. You know it's her by the clumps of paper clips stuck to the backs of her legs and tangled in her hair. Saelor and Jack have been up to no good again. At least this time it was only paper clips and not forks.

"Lucy!" you call ahead. "Wait up?"

She either doesn't hear you or is miffed about the paper clips and isn't in the mood to be social. You get it, having been on the receiving end of Saelor and Jack's pranks yourself. Their last attempt had you tied to your reading chair with red rope. You'd fallen asleep studying, and being the most savage friends ever, they tied you to the chair. They even used red rope just to torture you into trying to use your shoddy telekinesis. Luckily, Elwyn came to find you when you didn't show up to first class.

You're with the last group to arrive to breakfast. When you glance at the clock, you realize there's only ten minutes left to scarf down what is sure to be an unremarkable meal of now-cold oatmeal. You slide into your chair and spot Elwyn across from you. When he looks up, you wave, but he doesn't wave back or say a word.

Strange.

Turn to the next page.

4

Oh no. Did Saelor and Jack frame you for a prank on your best friend? It wouldn't be the first time. Those two are hilariously evil.

You lean forward to question him, but before you get a word out, Sal blurts, "We have a biology test today!" They drop their spoon, and their complexion goes pale. "I forgot to study!"

"It's not till second hour," Jack cuts in. "You'll be fine. Just study during English." He continues drowning his oatmeal in maple syrup.

"I can't! I've got a special session with the heights specialist first hour!" Sal buries their head in their hands.

Go on to the next page.

Everyone at Old Willow has the same academic class requirements, but each student also possesses a special ability—*a treasure trove of magic to be tamed*. The taming happens during special sessions with experts.

"Study while you're balancing up on the turret?" Saelor suggests, sharing a laugh with Jack.

You lean in closer to Sal. "You'll be fine. It's an easy unit—photosynthesis—you've got—"

Turn to page 7.

A blood-curdling scream erupts from somewhere in the old mansion.

Everyone freezes. There are looks of confusion and horror. But when another scream sounds, you and your fellow students jump up from the table and run toward the wailing.

The sound grows louder and louder until you reach the main library, where a group of students surround something—or someone.

In the chaos, you had fallen behind in the crowd, but now you are able to push your way toward the front.

It is here you stumble upon a strange scene:

The Headmistress is huddled on her knees on the library floor. Her hands cover her mouth, and, for the moment, she is silent.

Before her lies a student.

Still. Lifeless.

It's a dead body.

Your dead body.

*If you run away from the scene to gather your thoughts,
turn to the next page.*

*If you run back to your body and try to shake yourself awake,
because this must be another nightmare,
turn to page 14.*

Cobwebs and Cats

You quickly back away, but as you do, you pass through several students. It's like walking through a wall of thick cobwebs, stringy and sticky. You brush the invisible ick off your body while, at the same time, they collectively shiver and glance around the room as if looking for something they can't see.

"Nobody leaves," the Headmistress states gravely, not taking her eyes off your lifeless body. It takes you a minute to realize that the demand doesn't apply to you. It's both liberating and terrifying.

That's when it hits you. You can't leave. Not even if you wanted. At least, not as you once could. You lift your hands up in front of your face, examine your arms, look down at your body. You're misty and dull but also sort of shimmery. You are still wearing your school uniform, which is honestly a major bummer. "How?" you ask, but no one seems to notice. "Why?" You look left then right. "Why me?"

But your voice is a far-off thing.

You swallow, take a deep breath. "You're dead, Pearl," you say, not as convincing as you'd hoped to sound. You shake your head at yourself and squeeze your hands into fists.

You look down at your blurry, sort of glowy, self. "You are a ghost."

The weight sitting heavy on your chest sinks like a boulder to your stomach . . . or where your stomach would be.

Go on to the next page.

"If I'm dead"—*you are,* a forceful voice in your head confirms—"then why am I still here?"

Your eyes dart to the nearest door. Maybe you *don't* have to be here. You rush to the door, but when you grab for the knob, your hand passes right through the metal. You push your body full force into the door but only make it a fraction of the way through before you bounce back into the room. Instead of cobwebs, the door feels more like gelatin, cold and thick, moldable but still solid.

Just perfect.

Turn to the next page.

10

You're stuck in this stupid crowded room with your dead body for the foreseeable future. Instinctively, you back away to the opposite side of the room. When you feel the shelf of books behind you, you sink down the wall and onto the floor.

"This isn't happening," you say to yourself. "This cannot be happening."

Suddenly, you feel something push up next to you. Glancing over, you see it's Benedict, the Headmistress's cranky cat. He looks back at you with crystal yellow eyes as if he sees you.

You reach out to touch him and he bolts across the room and behind the curtains.

Great. You were always more of a dog person anyway.

Turn to page 12.

12

When Benedict jumps from the floor onto the windowsill, the curtains shift so you're able to see outside. You have a perfect view of the hedge maze. The maze swirls and sprawls a good acre or two. In the center is an old wooden gazebo. Vines crawl up and over it as if to further conceal the prize, such as it is. The hedges are always green even in the harsh winters that consume the old school, which sits in a remote forest up on the northernmost edge of Lake Willow. You used to think this was some sort of magic when most everything else went brown and dead come November. That is, until Elwyn unceremoniously burst your bubble a couple years ago and told you the hedges were a type of evergreen. Magic or not, it's your favorite place.

Or . . . it was.

You peek between the students still surrounding your body to get another look, but swiftly push your gaze back to the window. Too soon. Since you can't go to your thinking place, you suppose, this will have to do as the next best thing. So . . . you think.

You retrace your day from the moment you woke up yesterday. Breakfast was followed by a brisk walk with Elwyn. Morning classes were uneventful, as was lunch.

You recall trying to talk Jack and Saelor out of pranking Lucy with paper clips, but apparently you weren't very convincing.

Then afternoon classes.

Nothing stands out. Nothing at all.

"*Mother of Frankenstein*," you say to yourself. "How did this happen?" How did you end up a *ghost*? A wave of shivers washes over you.

Can ghosts creep themselves out? Because you're pretty sure you just did.

Go on to the next page.

The last thing you remember from the day before is dinner. Beef stew. You sat between Elwyn and Sal and, oddly, Constance was seated right across from you. She'd been late to arrive, and it had been the only open chair. Otherwise your mortal enemy never would have sat that close. Nothing makes sense.

You turn and face the room. Students have scattered into small groups. Miss Loveland, your English teacher, is comforting the Headmistress. Your body lies still and stiff on the floor.

You're going to have to face the grim reality of the situation: you're a ghost and it looks as if you've been murdered. But that knowledge alone isn't going to fix anything: you need to act. And fast. But solving a murder—your own murder!—isn't going to be easy. You wish you had help—except no one even knows you're in the room with them. You could try to find a way to communicate with your classmates . . . there must be a way, but who knows how long that will take to figure out? Every second you waste is another second the murderer gets away.

If you examine the scene for clues about your murder,
turn to page 18.

If you try to get someone's—anyone's—attention,
turn to page 26.

14

Reflections

You don't have a very good view from where you stand. All you can see is the black sleeve of your uniform sweater and the corner of your skirt.

It doesn't matter because it's not you.

It can't be you.

It's definitely you, your conscience—otherwise known as the annoying know-it-all in your head—chimes in.

You walk up right behind Jack and Sal. "Hey!" you say. They don't turn around.

Forget them.

You head toward Lucy and Saelor, who are standing with a few younger students.

"*Hello?*" you say, louder this time. But not one of them so much as glances your way.

"This isn't funny!" you shout at the room. "Stop ignoring me!" Still nothing. It's like you're not there.

You're not. Not really, anyway. Not as you once were.

"Shut up!" you shout at that pest in your head.

You try a door. But when you go to turn the knob, you're unable to grip it and your hand repeatedly passes through it.

You turn to face the room and march straight toward the line of students blocking you from the body on the floor. You make to push your way through so you can get a good look for yourself.

Instead, you walk through them. It's like traveling through thick sticky cobwebs and lingers longer than you'd like. A shiver jolts down your spine. When you glance back, no one's noticed.

But the fact that you just walked through several of your friends and fellow students, and the fact no one seems to hear you, doesn't bode well for who the lifeless body is that looks a lot like you lying at your feet.

Turn to the next page.

16

You kneel. Reaching your arm out, you notice your skin isn't fully solid and it's opalescent with a low glow to it.

Mother of Frankenstein.

You have to ignore it. With a tentative, fearful touch, you go to shake her shoulder. Your fingers pass straight through the other you. You try again. And again. Each time your hands go through as if there's nothing there. And each time you get a little more terrified.

"Wake up!" you try again, both hands attempting to grip the sides of your other self's face. But you're too forceful this time and lose your balance, falling forward so you tumble over against the floor onto your stomach. When you glance up something catches the light from under a chair.

You move in for a closer look.

It's a dagger.

There's blood on it.

Instinctively you look to your body and then reach to feel the back of your own head. What you feel is pretty normal but laced with static. You don't feel an injury.

And you're not able to make one out on the dead you on the floor.

Because that's it, isn't it? You're definitely dead.

Which makes you . . . a ghost?

Go on to the next page.

But how? When? Quickly, you recount the events of the day before, but nothing you did leads to you lying lifeless on the library floor. The problem is, your memories stop after dinner, when Constance, your mortal enemy, was, oddly, sitting across from you. After that it's all blackness.

Now, here you are.

You make your way to the mirror above the mantel. What does the ghost version of Pearl Margaret Maribel look like?

It takes a moment to work up the courage to look into the mirror, and when you do, nothing is as you expected.

You'd assumed you would see a transparent glowing version of yourself staring back. But all you see is the reflection of the library behind you.

And Constance, who stares right back at you.

A fraction of a second after your eyes meet, hers quickly veer away. But she seemed to see you, and the way she tried to avoid your gaze suggests she knows something.

The question is, will she spill what she knows if you find a way to confront her? It might be worth the try. Keep your enemies closer and all.

You have two ghost epiphanies: Constance can probably see you, maybe only in mirrors. And ghosts don't have reflections.

It's not much, but it's something helpful as you figure out this new life . . . er . . . death of yours. It also spurs all new questions. Does your gift of telekinesis still work? Could you use it to get that bloody knife out from under the chair?

If you try to confront your arch nemesis, Constance, turn to page 32.

If you try to use telekinesis to move the dagger out from under the chair, turn to page 37.

Curiouser and Curiouser

One of your favorite books is Mary Shelley's *Frankenstein*. In it, the monster leaves notes and clues behind for the doctor to find. In this instance, your death is the monster, and surely there have been clues left behind.

It makes sense to search near your body first, but with one glance and a shiver you quickly decide against it.

The outer edge of the library seems like the perfect place to start!

Walking the perimeter, you see that the room is mostly shelves and books. There are lamps and desks and comfortable chairs and couches organized into cozy reading areas. This is the school's main library and, for what is considered a small "quaint" school, it's a large space. Of course, the whole school is housed in an enormous old mansion.

Wall sconces with electric candles flicker and illuminate the space along with two grand chandeliers.

Go on to the next page.

Nothing out of the ordinary catches your attention; no clues, no books, no papers out of place. You make your way about halfway around the room when something stops you in your tracks.

Sawyer's knife case sits on a windowsill, partially concealed by the curtain.

Odd.

For a moment you forget you're a ghost and try to push the curtain aside and pick the case up. You nearly fall into the window.

Luckily, this is different from trying to hold or grab an object. You only make it a little way into the wall when the sticky cobwebs push you back from whence you came. Unlike the other sensation that was all cobwebs, this time the cobwebs are made of needles that prick every surface of your body.

You stumble onto the library floor.

Turn to the next page.

20

It takes a minute to shake off the pain and dizziness, but you focus back in on the dagger case. It's definitely Sawyer's—he's the only one who throws knives and, well, his initials are embossed along the spine of the case. It's his gift: knife throwing and archery. He claims he's been throwing sharp objects since before he could walk.

Sawyer practices in a remote area of the school grounds. There's no reason the knife case should be here in the library. Odder still, the leather case is open, and a single blade is missing. You look back at your body and then to the empty spot in the case where the dagger should be.

You jot this information down on a mental checklist you're compiling and continue searching. You move to inspect the mantel over the fireplace, but standing in your way is Elwyn.

At the sight of him, you're hit with a horrible truth: you're dead.

Of course, you knew this, but it didn't matter until just now when you realize you'll never be with your best friend again. Unless . . .

"Elwyn?" It comes out small and weak. "Elwyn," you say with more confidence.

He looks through you. It hurts far more than the cobweb needles.

"Hey," you say, tapping Elwyn on the shoulder. As you expect, your hand goes right through him like he's made of fog. But it's more like *you're* the cloud. You take a step back.

"Focus, Pearl . . . focus." If you get caught up in all the sad scary things being a ghost probably means, you'll never escape this room, let alone figure out how you ended up here in the first place.

Turn to page 22.

Giving Elwyn a last look, you move past him as he makes his way toward one of the windows where Lucy and Sal stand.

You examine the mantel. Framed photos of the first class to attend Old Willow and a larger portrait of the founder of the school sit in ornate frames flanking a mirror. Two red glass lamps sit opposite one another on each end. Moving along the old stone ledge, you see there's a crack in the lower right corner of the mirror with a small fragment missing.

"That wasn't broken yesterday . . ." The Headmistress is meticulous about these types of things. She runs a tight ship, Miss Loveland always says, which is her nice way of admitting the Headmistress is more a prison warden than a caring administrator.

A staff member would have noticed a broken mirror immediately and had it restored. That is, unless no one's had a chance to notice it yet.

Moving downward, there's a bit of ash spilling from the fireplace. You turn to move on when something in the back of the hearth makes you crouch down farther. There, between a couple of wood logs, is something shiny and yellow. Leaning in, you're able to make it out: it's the missing shard of mirror, and snagged to it is a yellow piece of fabric.

Go on to the next page.

The color and texture of the fabric is similar to the ribbon Constance wears in her hair every day.

It seems like if someone wanted to burn it or hide it, that could have been easily achieved. The scrap of mirror and fabric either fell into the fireplace by accident or someone left it there on purpose to be found.

You add these clues to your checklist: broken mirror, ash on the floor, and a yellow ribbon (probably—definitely—belonging to Constance). As you make your way along the rest of the perimeter and then zigzag around the interior, nothing seems to be out of the ordinary. All that's left is to inspect the scene of your death.

Taking a deep breath, you force yourself to stand tall. When you do, your feet temporarily leave the ground.

"Ah!" you shout, and drop back to the ground. It was only a few inches, but you've never floated before.

Turn to the next page.

24

To try again, you stand tall, stretching up onto your toes as high as you can.

Nothing happens.

Giving it another try, this time you close your eyes and imagine your feet lifting up off the floor.

Whoosh! Up, up, up you go!

Of course using your mind worked—you are telekinetic! But controlling your newfound gift of flight proves tricky as you drift like a balloon without direction.

You end up directly above your other self's body. Frozen dead eyes stare up at you. *Your* frozen dead eyes.

The sight startles you, and you drop like a boulder to the floor, veering to the side just in time to avoid landing on your lifeless body.

The floating must have taken a lot of energy out of you, because your arms and legs are like anvils. You do manage to move your head to the side. Avoiding your other self, you try to get a mouse's—or sassy cat's—eye view of the scene.

Go on to the next page.

There's a small tuft of Benedict's fur caught under the leg of the side table. A coin beneath the chair. And the missing knife from Sawyer's case!

Slowly regaining your strength, you inch your way closer to the dagger.

"Is that . . . ?" The last word refuses to escape your mouth. *Blood*.

Before you can grab the knife, several things happen in quick succession.

The Headmistress lets out another loud sob. There's a scuffle between several students, but you only make out Sawyer's spiky brown hair before all of the lights go out.

There's scrambling. Footsteps. Shouts. "Hey, what's going on?" The cat hisses. A door slams. Despite knowing it's probably fruitless, you reach all around for the dagger.

The lights switch back on.

No one's moved.

But the dagger's gone.

You immediately search out Sawyer. It is his dagger, after all. But he hasn't moved an inch. Still, it would be worthwhile to get a closer look—you did find his knife in the library with your blood on it. Those clues would make him prime suspect number one in Mary Shelley's eyes for sure.

Any good murder mystery would also advise you to look beyond the obvious. You *did* find a piece of broken mirror and a scrap of yellow fabric completely out of place. Examining the not-so-usual suspects might lead to even more clues.

If you further inspect suspect number one, Sawyer, turn to page 41.

If you search the others for someone wearing yellow or signs they broke a mirror, turn to page 45.

26

Anyone Home?

You search the space for your friends, but they're all scattered across the room. Nearest to you, sitting in a group of cushy leather chairs, is Constance with a few of her minions—the younger students who worship her for some unknown reason. She's not a friend, quite the opposite, but you decide to give it a try. You march right up to where she sits.

"Constance?" you say. "Can you see me?" She doesn't react. You lean right over her head and notice she's wearing a red ribbon around her long blond ponytail instead of her signature yellow. You shout, "Look at me!" For the briefest moment you swear her eyes pass over you, but when you say her name again, nothing.

You try to poke her on the shoulder, but your hand passes right through her.

You try again more forcefully.

Nothing.

You try once more because it's the strangest feeling—like sticking your fingers through a nest of thick cobwebs. Again, nothing. "Forget it."

Go on to the next page.

Taking a tentative step forward, you lean down and meet Miss Loveland face to face. She doesn't react. You wave your hand in front of her eyes. "Hello?" you say. "It's me, Miss Loveland. It's Pearl! I'm right here!"

She only stares right through you as she tends to the Headmistress, who is still in shock. There's no use trying to get through to her in that state.

Turn to the next page.

28

Crouching on the floor, you search the scene. It's difficult to see because of the pattern on the rug, but underneath your other self's head you find a small pool of blood.

You move lower to get a closer look, and when you do, you spot it: a dagger with blood on the handle shoved under the chair . . . and it looks a lot like one of Sawyer's.

You try to grab it but, of course, your hand passes through it.

Your gift is telekinesis . . . kind of. You can only move red objects. You try to focus on the red of the blood to move the knife, but either it's not red enough or your gift isn't as strong now that you're a ghost. You continue trying until you've exhausted yourself.

This is going nowhere.

You stand and again search the room. There, near one of the large, three-pane windows, stand Lucy, Elwyn, and Sal. Yes, Elwyn! Surely your closest friend, the person who knows you best in the world, will feel your presence, will hear you or see you or notice something.

But the closer you get, the stranger things feel.

Go on to the next page.

Lucy and Sal stand close to Elwyn, who leans against the windowsill, head down.

Sal speaks quietly. "Don't worry, we'll figure out what happened," they say, patting Elwyn softly on the shoulder. Sal clutches their signature red beanie—an accessory they rarely remove—in one hand as if out of respect.

Elwyn only sniffs in response.

Lucy stands quietly, sharing looks of concern with Sal as she continues to pluck paper clips from her legs, flicking them across the room so they're far enough away not to be pulled back to her.

You're not sure if it'll make things worse, but you move closer to Elwyn. His dark curly hair is tightly wound from the damp weather. You lean in, trying to make contact with his eyes, but they're squeezed closed. His cheeks are tinted pink and look warm under hot tears.

Turn to the next page.

30

And it hits you: you're dead.

Yes, that affects you. But you hadn't considered how it might affect your friends. Your family.

You start to take one of Elwyn's hands in yours, but as you edge closer, he quickly pulls his hand back and looks up. Did he feel something?

"Elwyn?" you say. "It's me. I'm here."

"I've gotta get out of here," he says, but not to you; he says it to Lucy and Sal. They share a concerned look, then usher him toward the door.

Your sadness turns to anger. How dare someone do this to you? How dare they make your friends go through this? You have to get out of here too.

But first, the dagger.

Go on to the next page.

Fear (mostly) gone, you quickly walk toward your body—you're going to pick that dagger up or at least push it into the middle of the room in a blaze of glory, an aha moment reveal. But before you take so much as three steps, something crashes to the floor across the room. Everyone's heads turn toward the noise.

On an uppermost shelf sits Benedict, meticulously grooming his tail. On his way up, the rascal kicked several antique volumes off the edge, causing a domino effect and a book avalanche. You could swear that dumb cat knows exactly what he's doing.

You refocus and march straight for the dagger. But when you get there, it's gone.

"Everyone to your rooms immediately," the Headmistress says gravely.

The room scrambles in commotion and movement. Now's your chance to escape this room! But which way? Someone has that dagger and it's going in one of two directions. The students all shuffle to the east door that leads to the dormitories. Miss Loveland and the Headmistress walk to the west exit and the teachers' quarters.

If you quickly follow the last student out the door before it closes, turn to page 51.

If you decide to follow Miss Loveland and the Headmistress to see where they are headed, turn to page 56.

Keep Your Enemies Close

You turn and face Constance head on. It only takes a couple of strides to reach where she sits.

You lean down so you're eye to eye with your nemesis. This is the girl who isn't afraid to tell you she hates you to your face. The girl who uses her gifts to make your chair slide out from under you. To make your soup spill into your lap. To make doors lock you in or out.

If someone had told you the girl with the gift of communicating with inanimate objects would bully you with her gift, you'd have laughed, because how the creeps could someone possibly do that? Well, leave it to Constance to find a way. Not only does she communicate with all the things that surround you day and night, but she also convinces them to animate! They're like her own personal puppets of torture.

As you stare into her icy blue eyes, something suddenly occurs to you.

It's no secret she and Elwyn used to be good friends before you arrived at Old Willow. And it's no secret she believes it was you who pulled them apart. Was this her way of getting rid of you once and for all? Can she make daggers fly into unsuspecting students walking through the library?

No . . . Her gifts don't work like that. You don't think they do, anyway.

Constance sighs loudly as if she's reading your thoughts. You take a step back. Are you an inanimate object now that you're a ghost? Can she hear every word you think?

"Constance?" you say. "Can you see me?"

She rolls her eyes.

"Constance!"

She tightens the red ribbon securing her long blond ponytail.

"Can you hear me? Look at me! Say something to me!"

Constance clears her throat and calls Benedict, the Headmistress's creepy cat, over to her. Of course, she's the only one he likes other than the Headmistress and the cook who feeds him more scraps than he deserves. The little gnat curls up in her lap and she smiles. For some reason this pushes you over the edge.

Turn to page 34.

"I know you can see me!" You slam your fist against the arm of Constance's chair. Your hand flies through it, which makes you even angrier.

As you turn away from Constance, your eyes dart around the room. To Elwyn, your best friend. To Miss Loveland and the Headmistress. To the many groups of students all surely speculating.

No one can see you. No one can help you. And you can't do anything about it.

You turn back toward the mirror only to be reminded you don't even have a reflection. You barely exist.

Your hands squeeze into fists. There's so much anger and confusion and sadness trapped inside your cloud of a body and you can't do anything with any of it. Without thinking, you lean in and punch the mirror. It rattles loudly, threatening to fall off the wall and shatter.

The room collectively reacts to the noise. A couple of people gasp. Several glance in your direction.

Benedict leaps from Constance's lap and dives to the floor. He runs and hides under a table.

Your breath is heavy as you examine your hand and calm down. It's just as misty as the rest of your body, but you actually made contact with something. Why didn't your hand pass through the mirror and the wall behind it that time?

You look around. Everyone has gone back to whatever it was they were doing. Perhaps the noise wasn't as loud as it felt.

Only Constance stares at the mirror and where you stand. That anger wells up again. *Wait—anger! That's it!*

Go on to the next page.

You quickly make your way to the dagger—maybe you can use the force of your anger to move it out from under the chair. But when you crouch down to move it, it's gone!

"What the . . . ?" You glance around the room. Anyone could have it.

You walk back toward Constance and try to move a book on the table next to her, but it seems your energy is drained and your hand slips through it. You head to the window and think about how you can't get outside. Your frustration builds and you quickly try to harness it and push the window open. It doesn't budge, but you do leave a small smudge of contact against the glass.

New ghost rule: Ghosts can use anger to touch things. Sometimes.

Perhaps if you rest a while, you can try again. If you can get as angry as you were a moment ago, you might just be able to bust through the door and escape.

Turn to the next page.

Unbridled Anger

While you wait for your energy to recoup, you try out other emotions to see if any has the same effect on objects. Sadness comes easily. You approach the nearest table and flick the pencil a student must have left behind. It goes flying.

It's more difficult right now to become happy, but you feel it's safe to assume it would work too.

You go back to anger, which is ever-present under the surface. You set your sights on the door.

Then you look to your other self, where she lies so sadly, so plainly on the floor.

The heat of unbridled anger boils from every fiber of your existence, whatever that may be at the moment.

You run as fast as you can toward the door and slam fists first into it. Your body goes through several layers of wood. It's thick and sticky and feels like the the prick of needles. But you bounce back into the library.

Defeated, you slide down the wall, pull your knees to your chest, and scream.

The two sconces that flank one of the school's many secret passageways flicker. No one seems to notice.

You try again, but it doesn't happen a second time. What does happen is you realize that passageway could be your escape route.

You realize you've been going about this the wrong way. You don't need to go through a door, you need to find an alternative door. Benedict's cat door might just work.

*If you take the secret passage,
turn to page 90.*

*If you go through the cat door,
turn to page 94.*

You've Still Got It . . . Sort of

"Let's see if I've still got it."

Your gift, and the reason you were sent to the Old Willow Boarding School for Gifted Children, is telekinesis. Well, unpredictable telekinesis. The problem was, you could control only red objects with your mind. Even worse, you weren't very good at it. You were constantly breaking red items by accident at home and moving things at school, where you were deemed a distraction to other students.

The final straw was when, while traveling in the car with your father, you accidentally forced a red bicycle into the middle of the road. Your car hit it, but luckily no one was riding it.

That was it.

Your mother heard from a friend who talked to a teacher who had seen an obscure ad in a tiny newspaper about the mostly hidden, very quiet, forest-surrounded, quite expensive, and even more exclusive school at the uppermost edge of Lake Willow.

After countless interviews, tests, and letters of recommendation, you were accepted.

Turn to the next page.

And here you are. A ghost.

You lie on your stomach and scoot as close as you can to the dagger while also avoiding your dead body because it's just weird. There isn't a lot of blood showing, the way the knife is angled, but you've accidentally moved smaller red objects before so it's worth a try.

You concentrate on the red stain. You envision it moving, sliding along the floor until it's in plain sight.

Nothing happens.

"Come on, Pearl. *Come on!*"

Move the dagger.

Move the dagger.

Move. The. Dagger.

It wobbles. Then stops.

You keep at it and do manage to make the corner of the dark red blanket thrown over the chair shift, but that's it.

Fine. You get up and look around the room. "If I can't get the knife to move, I'll move something else in here. Get someone's attention."

Go on to the next page.

There's got to be something bright red in this room. Something you can really make move or shake to get someone's attention.

There's a meow at your feet. Benedict. The insufferable cat's collar is red. Perhaps . . .

No.

"I'm not desperate enough to fling the cat across the room," you say. Benedict swipes his sharp claws at your foot. "Yet."

Then you spot it: the perfect object. The red glass lamp on the mantel will do just perfectly.

You move toward the closest chair so you can sit and really concentrate.

Where you sit, your dead body is in sight. You figure you'll practice moving the dagger a bit more before you really go for it with the lamp.

But when you lean forward to get a good view of the knife, it's gone!

You need to alert someone. That lamp needs to fly off the mantel.

Turn to the next page.

Someone Notice!

You move until you're about a foot away from the lamp. Too far or too close and you lose focus. You concentrate on the lamp. It's bright cherry red and the glass is not quite translucent. You imagine it sliding with ease to the right and off the edge of the mantel.

As you concentrate, the dim light of the lamp flickers. The lamp's symmetric twin on the other side of the mantel also flickers, as does the nearest chandelier. It seems that the energy you're pushing outward is affecting more than just the lamp, which now shakes and teeters.

"Come on, come on!" With a final surge of emotion, you manage to push the lamp over the edge of the mantel. It shatters spectacularly. The room collectively gasps and looks toward the fireplace.

"Yes!" you shout, but your triumph is short-lived—the red glass shattering triggers a memory.

Yesterday you accidentally broke a similarly red object by pushing it off a shelf with your mind. But that object was not an insignificant lamp. It was an urn. The founder of the Old Willow Boarding School for Gifted Children's urn, to be exact. The bright red had caught your eye and before you could stop it, the urn had moved off the side of the shelf and shattered on the floor, ashes and all. The Headmistress was livid.

But the memory fades to black there.

You observe the room. Constance appears uneasy and refuses to look directly at the mess you just made. Elwyn's eyes dart from corner to corner as if he's trying to spot something he can't see. Low chatter erupts.

As you're trying to find something else to shatter, the Headmistress shouts, "Everyone to your rooms! Now!"

You want to stay close to Elwyn, get through to him, but he takes off fast. You follow, but just as you reach the door you stop dead.

It feels unnatural to leave your body behind.

If you follow Elwyn, turn to page 96.

If you stay with your body, turn to page 100.

Sawyer the Knife Thrower

Sawyer Saint James. Knife thrower. Archer.

How he ended up at Old Willow is an area of speculation and myth. It's been both downplayed and overexaggerated. It's one of those things where the truth probably lies somewhere in between.

The story most commonly told is that Sawyer would climb out of his crib during the night and crawl to the kitchen. He would scale the counter and steal the steak knives, which he would use to pin his stuffed animals to his nursery wall.

It only progressed from there.

Turn to the next page.

42

As he got older, his skills rapidly developed beyond his young understanding. Sawyer would shoot arrows at the neighborhood children's bike tires from his roof. He would throw daggers from behind trees on garbage pickup day and spill trash in yards to attract raccoons and bears. When his knives were confiscated, he would turn to darts, whittle spears from branches, or throw pushpins if he had to. Supposedly, the final blow for Sawyer was when he was caught charging his schoolmates to take turns spinning on a wheel he'd fashioned from old barn wood. One dollar to spin, and a dollar for every knife that *didn't* miss.

The overexaggerated story is that Sawyer indeed missed that day.

The downplayed story is that no one was hurt, but every parent demanded Sawyer be either sent away or arrested.

And here he is. At the Old Willow Boarding School.

A single dagger missing from his knife case. Had he missed last night in the library? Or had he hit his target?

You move to where Sawyer sits with Jack and a couple of other boys a year ahead of you. Like most of the students, they're speculating about your fate.

"She probably just tripped and hit her head or something," one of the boys says.

"Nah, I bet that creepy Mr. Fitzherbert did her in for something stupid like not wiping her muddy shoes!" the other one says. They share a laugh but realize what they're laughing about and quickly quiet down.

Sawyer doesn't join in. In fact, he's not saying much at all. He is intent on nervously tapping his fingers against the side table next to him. And he keeps glancing at Lucy, who is across the room comforting Elwyn. She avoids his stares.

Go on to the next page.

There are no torn scraps of yellow fabric missing on Sawyer's clothing and his hair isn't mussed or disheveled. His shoes are newly polished. The only thing suspicious about Sawyer is that his tie is a bit looser than normal and his knife case is oddly placed in the library. And, well, there's the small detail of one of the knives missing—hidden under a chair near your dead body and with what you assume is your blood on it.

The same dagger that disappeared as mysteriously as Sawyer arrived here at Old Willow.

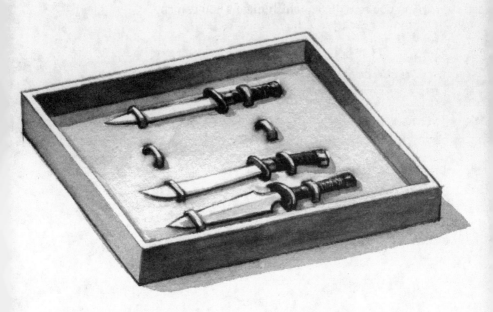

Turn to the next page.

Suspicious? Yes. Does it make Sawyer guilty? Not yet, but he's suspect number one on your list. Why he would murder you, though, you haven't a clue.

You intend to find out. But how?

You're not gleaning any new clues the longer you're trapped in the library. Why in the world is Sawyer's dagger case here? And what's going on between him and Lucy?

If only you could tap into Sawyer's thoughts. But that's not your gift. No one currently at Old Willow reads thoughts. You silently go over all your friends' gifts and when you get to Elwyn the answer smacks you in the face. If you could find a way to time travel along with Elwyn, you could go back and follow Sawyer's movements.

But maybe he's not guilty at all. You shrug to yourself. There's a whole room full of possible suspects surrounding you.

And you're a ghost, which means you can spy.

If you try to hitchhike with Elwyn, time travel to before you were murdered, and follow Sawyer, turn to page 58.

If you choose to do some ghost spying to find the killer before they strike again, turn to page 64.

Coming Up Yellow Daisies

"Something yellow . . . something yellow . . ." You scan the room with a keen eye for flashes of yellow fabric. You have no idea how the mirror was broken or when you were mortally attacked. The murderer could still be wearing the yellow piece of clothing in question.

Red used to be your favorite color. That is, before your telekinesis surfaced and you quickly realized red objects were all you could attempt to control. Red was then associated with struggle, horror, and incompetence.

Yellow became your new favorite color. That is, until you noticed Constance wore a yellow ribbon every day.

You are currently in your all-black era. It feels more appropriate than ever.

You make your way across the library to the bookstack ladder—getting more of an aerial view will be especially helpful. But when you go to climb the first rung, your legs slip right through the ladder.

"Ugh!" You kick the ladder, and, thanks to your anger, this time your foot makes contact. "Ow! Stupid ghost legs!"

You're angry and could probably try to climb the ladder, but it seems needlessly risky.

You do attempt your new ghost floating skill, but the moment you reach more than six inches off the ground, things get unsteady.

Instead, you keep it familiar and simply walk around the room, taking note of every scrap of yellow you see. Surprisingly, there's a lot. Which is when you realize you have a problem. Old Willow's uniform colors are navy, forest green, and . . . yellow.

The odds are officially stacked against you.

Everyone has a bit of yellow on, including Miss Loveland and the Headmistress.

Just great.

Turn to the next page.

46

Lucy.

You get a good look at her sweater vest, which is still littered with paper clips. The problem is, it's knit, and the fabric caught on the mirror was smooth, not very frayed.

On your way to inspect the Headmistress's blouse, Jack catches your eye. His arm is in a sling. You're sure he wasn't wearing it yesterday. And it's yellow!

"Mother of Frankenstein . . ."

Go on to the next page.

Jackson "Jack" Miller claims to have lived and died multiple past lives. Because of this, his gifts are wide and varied. These gifts are also unpredictable and come and go without warning. He speaks countless languages, can pick locks, convince others to do his bidding, predict the weather, and contort his body into the smallest kitchen cabinet in the school.

Jack can't recall exactly what gift-related mischief got him sent to Old Willow. He had broken into the principal's office at his old school, made a twenty-minute phone call to the Falkland Islands, talked a bus of Girl Scouts into giving him a ride to the airport, and was climbing in the luggage bay of a plane by the time he was finally caught. He arrived at Old Willow by police escort.

Could Jack have something to do with your death? It's worth investigating further.

The sling is made from a scrap of yellow fabric so it's impossible to tell if it's been torn or not. You listen in to see if you can get any information about it.

"What do you think happened?" Sal asks Jack, their voice low and serious.

"I don't know," Jack says in a monotone. Is his tone sad or is it steady because he's trying to pass off a lie?

"I bet it was one of those heavy poetry books she's always climbing up to reach. I warned her not to go climbing the ladder alone!" Lucy sobs. But Lucy is also a talented actress. Sal puts their arm around her for comfort, before realizing the bracelet they're wearing has metal on it.

Their arm sticks to Lucy's magnetic shoulder.

"Oh! I'm sorry!" Sal says.

"Not your fault." Lucy recites those words several times a day.

Jack jumps into action and, using his non-sling arm, pulls the bracelet off Sal's wrist and sets it on the table. He winces with the motion.

"What did you do to your arm, Jack?" you ask, though you know he can't hear you.

Turn to the next page.

You take a quick inventory: Sawyer's wearing a yellow tie; Lucy a yellow knit vest; Jack a yellow sling; and the Headmistress a yellow blouse. Countless others have yellow on, but too little to have left a torn piece attached to the broken mirror.

But who knows what everyone was wearing yesterday? Or last night? Anyone could have made a quick change.

Ugh. This is much harder than you thought it would be.

You continue making your way toward the Headmistress. She now sits on the chair nearest to your body. The same chair under which the dagger disappeared. Her light yellow blouse is a silky material, but only the collar and a tinge of the cuffs are visible underneath her blazer. You go in for a closer look, but Benedict leaps into the Headmistress's lap and you've missed your chance.

He hisses at you.

"Shhh . . . shhh . . . my little prince," the Headmistress coos.

Even though you're pretty sure you no longer have a stomach, it turns several times over.

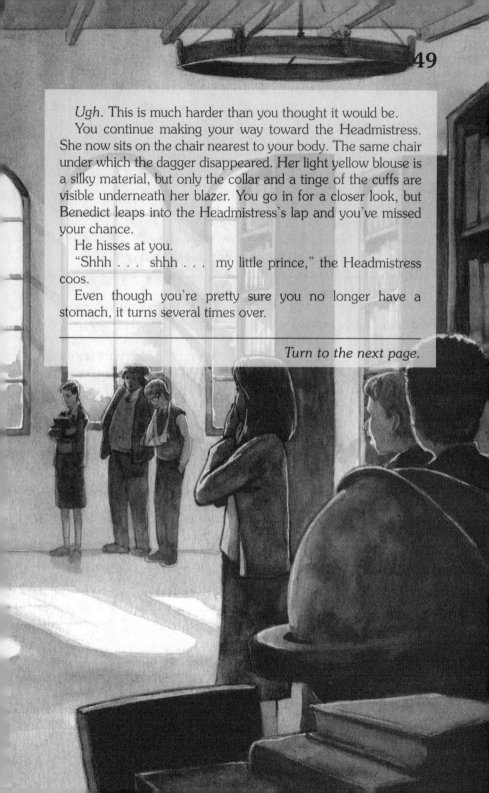

Turn to the next page.

50

You need a new tactic. Glancing from yellow clothing item to yellow clothing item, they're so different. Different shades, different textures . . .

Wait . . .

" . . . I just need to compare them to the original!"

You quickly and precariously float to the fireplace. A familiar smell hits you as you approach the hearth.

"What the . . . ?"

A fire's been lit.

"Mother of Frankenstein, when did that happen?"

But it doesn't really matter because the evidence is gone.

The Headmistress stands and walks to the center of the room. "Students, everyone to your dorms. Now."

"Finally!" you say. You cannot get out of this library fast enough. And it seems you're not the only one. Everyone takes off out the two opposite doors. Students head to their dorm rooms and the teachers head to wherever teachers go when they aren't looking after students.

"Which way?" You begin to panic. On one hand, the Headmistress is wearing that yellow blouse and she was the one who found your body.

But Constance has been your enemy since day one, and all of a sudden, on the day you die, she stops wearing her yellow ribbon?

If you try to get a better look at the Headmistress's yellow blouse, turn to page 68.

If you search Constance's room for a torn yellow ribbon, turn to page 72.

Lucy the Magnetic

In your rush to get out the door, instead of running, you float! Well, *glide* more like, just above the floor. You're so excited by this new ghost development, you don't realize how close you've gotten to Lucy. She's the student you stuck closest to in order to get out of the library, but now you see you're *literally* stuck to her. Like a magnet. You're floating but Lucy is *pulling* you.

She pulls you out the door of the library, down the hallway, and up the stairs to the east common room. You're now one of the hordes of items constantly trailing behind the poor girl.

Lucy grew up in a small factory town. She talks about how the noises from the smokestacks and machinery used to lull her to sleep. During the summers the heat and humidity from the factory were unbearable, but there was a river that wound along the outskirts of Lucy's neighborhood.

Sure, there were warning signs all around the river. And sure, her parents told her to never get in the water. But it was so hot.

Lucy only took a quick swim to cool off. Nothing was strange at first, but slowly over time, metal objects were attracted to her. It started with the doorknob to her bedroom "sticking" to her hand. Then she struggled to get off her bike. Things like sewing needles and eating utensils and her school locker became troublesome. The final blow, and why her parents had no choice but seek out Old Willow, was when Lucy visited her father's hardware store.

Something must have clicked. Perhaps being exposed to so much metal at once? The moment she walked through the door, nearly every saw, nail, screw, and hammer flew toward her. It's a miracle she wasn't killed. And luckily the shop was empty. Lucy has a large scar over her right eye from a screwdriver slicing her forehead.

She was immediately accepted into the Old Willow Boarding School.

Turn to page 53.

You trail behind Lucy as she walks through the common room and toward the dorm rooms. Lucy's long black braids swing with each step, and you notice there's a thumbtack stuck in one and a couple of paper clips in the other.

You try everything you can think of to detach. Dropping to the floor doesn't work. And floating up as high as you can makes you into a balloon being pulled over Lucy's head. Ghosts must be magnetic because the pull Lucy has on you is more than you can control.

Lucy's dorm is like a closet of curiosities riddled with odds and ends picked up from one side of the school to the other. There are large magnets bolted to the wall that have an opposite attraction to her. She uses them to help remove metal from her body when she returns each day.

When Lucy makes her way down the hall to the bathroom, the heavy door quickly closes behind her, finally cutting the invisible magnetic cord between the two of you. You rush away but see she left the door to her room open. You don't want to get stuck, but you need to search for clues about your death.

Turn to the next page.

54

You go for it, but you only have minutes until she returns. In a rush, you search among the chaos of Lucy's bedroom. Everything is in piles, impossible to sort through. "Why can't I just pick things up?" Frustration wells in your chest. This isn't fair. Your eyes prick with invisible angry tears.

"Ugh!" You shove an already open drawer closed. "Whoa—" you freeze, then try again with an open cabinet. It doesn't budge.

"Nothing makes sense!" you shout, kicking at a padlock on the floor.

You focus on your anger, feel it build in your gut. Then you shove the desk chair. It moves! Using the same method, you open a jewelry box. Then close the lid of a chest.

"Nice!"

You're exhausted, but you give this trick a try on Lucy's closet door. You manage to turn the knob and open it a crack, but that's it. Apparently there's a limit to how many objects you can manipulate with your emotions before you're drained.

Go on to the next page.

The distant sound of clanking metal alerts you to Lucy's return.

You quickly take off down the hall and to the common room, where several students are gathered. Perhaps, instead of searching for a needle in a haystack, or a dagger in a mansion, you should test something out. If Lucy's gifts affected you, what if the same will happen with other students? Whose gifts could you use to your advantage?

Getting a bird's-eye view of the school grounds could lead you to a clue. Sal would be the one to help you with that.

Constance walks by and not so subtly glances in your direction. If only you could get her to crack. But the only time you've ever seen her upset is when Saelor and Jack pranked her with bugs in her bed—Constance's one fear.

"That's it!"

You need to tap into Saelor's gifts.

If you try to borrow Sal's gifts,
turn to page 76.

If you try to tap into Saelor's gifts,
turn to page 79.

No One Can Be Trusted

Students scatter.

There are three doors out of the library. Two lead toward the dorms and student common areas. The other door goes in the direction of the communal areas, classrooms, and offices.

Someone has that dagger or knows where it is, because daggers don't just disappear into thin air. Well, except when Rosie Derringer attended Old Willow. Her gift was that of a poltergeist. She often made objects move and disappear to other places in the school, but she was transferred last year.

Since you're not able to open doors, you choose the closest one and follow Miss Loveland and the Headmistress out of the library. It feels strange to leave your body all alone, but you suppose you won't be needing it anytime soon.

Go on to the next page.

They walk in stunned silence until Miss Loveland says, "Headmistress." Her expression is heavy with concern as she continues, "Shall I call the authorities? I know you prefer to keep a low profile, but this . . . A student has been . . ."

"I'm well aware of the severity of the situation and I have it under control." The Headmistress's tone is cold, distant. She's probably still in shock.

"Yes, ma'am." Miss Loveland nods, her shoulder-length brown hair swaying with the motion. "May I walk you up? Would you like a cup of tea?" You can tell she wants to ask more.

"No, I'm fine." The Headmistress stops where the hallway forks. "Thank you for your concern. Mr. Fitzherbert will make arrangements and I will contact the necessary parties."

"Please—if there's anything I can do to help."

"Actually, would you share the news with the rest of the teaching staff and remind them their discretion is expected, especially considering the sensitive nature of the situation?"

"Yes, Headmistress." Miss Loveland nods again and turns to the left.

The Headmistress turns to the right.

You look back and forth between them, unsure of who to follow.

If you follow the Headmistress,
turn to page 84.

If you follow Miss Loveland,
turn to page 87.

Duck, Duck, Poke

Elwyn's gift is time travel. Uncontrolled time travel. He's horrible at it. The problem is he often only travels short distances into the past. It's usually completely unintentional or spurred on by stress. But you can use both of these things to your advantage.

Elwyn's gift surfaced around age nine. He would go out to play and not come back for hours or return a town over and call his parents to pick him up. He kept getting in trouble for running away and then in more trouble for telling silly stories about time travel. The older he got, the more frequent the episodes. Sometimes he'd only be gone for moments. Other times hours. Once he disappeared from school, materialized in the center ring of a traveling circus, spent a good twenty-four hours as a clown wrangler, and then returned during math class the next day.

The main problem with Elwyn's gift was that he had no control over it. He never knew when he might disappear and return or where he'd end up in between.

His parents finally believed him when they saw it with their own eyes. His father was chiding him for his frequent disappearing when a second Elwyn appeared right outside the kitchen window.

Go on to the next page.

You spot Elwyn. He's on the other side of the room, walking around slowly, head down as if looking for something. When he stops and stares at the wall you realize what's going on—he's trying to time travel.

Always one step ahead of you!

But it doesn't seem to be working. On the rare occasion he's been able to time travel on purpose, it's usually from someplace comfortable—his bed or chair—where he can really concentrate.

"Students," the Headmistress says, "everyone to your dorms. Now."

Elwyn's right next to the door and slips out before you get a chance to move his way.

"No!" you shout. "Wait!"

Turn to the next page.

60

You rush as fast as you can to the door, but it's too late. Nearly. In your fear of missing your chance to escape and anger at not getting to Elwyn in time, something snaps. Out of habit you go to push the door open, but instead of your hand passing through it, you make contact! You shove the door open enough to get through.

It's as if the energy of your emotions traveled to your hands and then made them more solid. Whatever it was, you're going to try to use it to stress Elwyn out enough to make him time travel.

You speed-float your way down the hall and right behind your best friend. All you want is to muss his curly hair and wrap him in a bear hug and tell him everything is fine.

Instead, you push all those feelings into energy that surges down to your hand, and you poke him. HARD.

"Ow!" He skids to a halt. He looks around and sees nothing.

You poke him again. And again.

He takes off to his dorm room, but you stay right on him, continuously poking and prodding.

Before he even makes it to the common room—ZAP.

Elwyn starts to fade. You've seen him do it before. He goes sort of staticky and then disappears. Using what energy you have left to grab something, you cling onto his arm for dear life before it's too late.

Elwyn has tried to explain the sensation of time traveling, but he always struggles. "There's just nothing to compare it to," he says.

You can now concur. Time travel is being squeezed, pushed, and stretched all at once.

Turn to page 63.

You arrive in Elwyn's bedroom and it's morning. You realize, by the fact that there are two Elwyns—one sleeping in bed and the other standing and wearing his uniform—that you've indeed time traveled.

Elwyn is much better at finding his bearings than you are. He quickly jumps into action and checks the clock and calendar. Then he runs out the door.

You also check the clock and calendar. It's early that same morning. Before your body was found. Possibly before your death.

You bolt out the door after Elwyn but stop in your tracks. Splitting up would cover more ground—you could check the school for suspicious activity the morning of your death.

On the other hand, you're not even sure Elwyn knows you're there and you'll need him to travel back to the present.

You think.

*If you follow Elwyn,
turn to page 104.*

*If you go off on your own to search the school,
turn to page 109.*

Whodunit?

"I heard she snuck into the kitchen to make hot chocolate but accidentally put rat poison instead of sugar in her cup!" a first-year girl whispers to another.

Sam, who's a year ahead of you, mumbles to a kid sitting next to him, "I bet she choked on chewing gum. It happens. And it's not pretty." Sam's gift is compulsive lying with the ability to make people believe him without doubt.

"Brutal," the student next to him says.

You sneak over to a table where several of the prophetic seers are sitting. They're passing a paper around, writing notes to one another. The last line reads: *She comes back to haunt us.* You gasp.

But the next student writes: *As a mouse.* They collectively nod.

Their predictions are rarely correct.

"Students, go straight to your dorm rooms. Now," the Headmistress says, cutting into your sleuthing.

Go on to the next page.

All the students take off, their conversations getting louder the farther they get away from the Headmistress.

You take this opportunity to escape the library. As you're slipping out the door, you notice Sawyer lagging behind. You're pushed out into the hallway just as he's retrieving his dagger case. Sawyer discreetly slips the case into his book bag. He either knew it was there the whole time or just spotted it.

Students aren't allowed to have deadly objects or weapons, or anything that might cause harm, outside of their specialized classes.

In the spirit of spying, you settle in the common area. It's without doubt where you will hear the most chatter. As you suspected, most of the students did not go straight to their dorms despite the Headmistress's orders.

You approach Jack and Sal. Jack is going back and forth between speaking English and French, but you're able to make out, "*Mais oui*, Saelor and I pranked Lucy last night. Nothing seemed unusual."

Sal leans in, pushing their wavy black hair behind their ears. "Did you two go by the library though?"

Turn to the next page.

"No, we only snuck into Lucy's room." Jack shakes his head. "What about you?"

"I've got nothing. I did hear from Lucy that Constance was seen near the library. But Constance says she wasn't anywhere near the library and that she went to bed early." Sal shrugs.

"A likely story," you say, even though you know they can't hear you.

Sawyer isn't anywhere to be seen.

You glance around and notice Constance is talking with Lucy. Constance, your mortal enemy. The girl who claims you stole her best friend, Elwyn, and has used her gift to torment you ever since. If anyone had a motive to get rid of you, it's her.

You approach them to find Lucy is crying. "I was so mean! I can't believe our last conversation was such a stupid argument!" Lucy sobs.

"It's okay . . . I'm sure she knew you didn't mean it . . ." Constance tries to console Lucy. You're surprised. You didn't know it was in her nature.

"I don't even remember what we were arguing about. It's fine, Lucy, really," you say.

"But I yelled at her, Constance. She borrowed my sweater. I thought she lost it, but it was under my bed. I found it this morning!"

Oh yeah. "Poor Lucy. That argument is the least of my worries right now." You move on.

Go on to the next page.

Elwyn sits alone by the fireplace writing in a notebook. You lean over his shoulder but only make out the words *why* and *how* before there's a loud, urgent knock at the school's main doors downstairs. Elwyn slams his notebook shut.

Everyone rushes toward the windows to get a glimpse of who it is. Everyone except Constance. She edges her way around a corner and disappears.

You're torn. Everyone seems excited to see who's at the door— no one stops by the Old Willow Boarding School for Gifted Children. You have to take a boat to reach it, for one.

But . . . "Constance, what are you up to?" you wonder. You'd really like to find out.

If you follow Constance, turn to page 111.

If you go see who's at the front door, turn to page 114.

The Headmistress's Turret

Following the Headmistress feels wrong, off limits, sort of scandalous.

You like it.

And after all, she's the one who found you and, well, if anyone is skilled at keeping secrets about the school or its students, it's her. The Old Willow Boarding School is the Headmistress's lifeblood, her legacy. She might not have founded the school herself, but she molded it into something that serves a purpose and is somehow both more exclusive and more mysterious than before. She's been known to go to great lengths to protect its reputation and, by association, her own.

You follow her down several winding halls, up the back stairs, up a much steeper twisty spiral staircase, and through her locked door. You now find yourself in forbidden territory.

The Headmistress's turret. Her tower. The place where all cellphones are kept under lock and key.

All morning she's sat over your body, bereaved, intermittently sobbing. But now? She seems completely normal. Almost cold. Was it an act or is she all cried out? Is she still in shock?

As you follow close behind, you try to examine her yellow blouse for any snags or tears. She always wears her hair up in a neat bun, which gives you a good view of the collar. It's meticulously pressed. Next, you float around so you're in front of the Headmistress. You get a good look at the front of her blouse and the cuffs of her sleeves.

Not a thread is out of place.

This doesn't completely exonerate her from the yellow fabric and mirror clue, but until you can catch her without her jacket on, you decide to table it and move on to other suspicions.

Like, for instance, the mysteries that are sure to dwell in her office.

The Headmistress removes an antique metal key from her pocket and unlocks her door. You can't wait to snoop, but the moment you glide over the threshold, a forgotten memory flashes before your eyes.

Turn to page 70.

70

"Mother of Frankenstein!" you shout, then smack your hand over your mouth, forgetting the Headmistress can't hear you. You'd laugh if the memory wasn't so strange.

You were here. In this very room. Yesterday.

But only students who get into trouble grace these walls, and you never got into trouble. Try as you may to recall why you were in the Headmistress's office, the memory goes dark.

You walk around the large circular room trying to jog your brain into more details, but you stop dead when the Headmistress removes a bundle from her pocket. When she sets the heavy object on her desk, the handkerchief it's wrapped in falls off to reveal the bloody dagger.

"What the . . . ?" you say in shock.

She wraps the dagger back up and locks it in one of her desk drawers.

Before you can fully register what you've witnessed, there's a loud knock at the door. Without being invited, Mr. Fitzherbert bursts into the room.

"Madam! What are we to do?" he shouts.

The Headmistress stands and slams her hands onto her desk. "Shhh! Shut the door, Fitzherbert!"

Go on to the next page.

He closes the door and approaches her desk. "Forgive me, madam, but we could have a murder on our hands. This could ruin the school!"

"You think I don't realize that?" She unlocks the drawer and pulls out the dagger. "That's why I'm holding onto this—it could come in handy."

"But what do we do? How do we keep this from getting out? The girl . . . she's . . . she's still . . ."

"Calm yourself, Fitzherbert, my heavens. You act like we've never had a student die before."

Wait. *What?*

The Headmistress locks the dagger back up and approaches Mr. Fitzherbert. "We will interview every student who was close to Pearl or recently seen with her. I'm good at a lot of things, but getting people—especially children—to talk is one of my specialties." She grins.

Mr. Fitzherbert nods emphatically. They leave to get started.

You are left alone in the Headmistress's office with the dagger.

. . . and the cellphones.

*If you choose to try to get your hands on the dagger,
turn to page 121.*

*If you decide to break into the cellphone drawer,
turn to page 125.*

Most everyone, including Constance, is in the common room speculating.

"I was able to climb to the top bookshelf without anyone noticing and I got a really good view," Sal says to Saelor. "Pearl was face up and there was a pool of blood underneath her head."

"That's horrible, Sal," Saelor says. "Did you see a weapon?"

Sal shakes their head no.

"Good thing you weren't caught."

"Eh . . . it's not the first time I managed to get up to the ceiling unnoticed."

Fair. Sal is not only a genius climber, but also eerily silent.

Saelor goes on to tell Sal that she sent a colony of sugar ants to look for signs of a struggle or evidence, but they came up empty.

You pass through the space unnoticed. Well, mostly unnoticed. Benedict has followed you the whole way up and keeps clawing at your heels. Insufferable cat!

Go on to the next page.

When you get to Constance's dorm room, to your surprise, you don't have to work very hard to open the door. Stranger still, it closes behind you, shutting Benedict out. "Thanks for that," you say, laughing to yourself. "Weird old house."

You begin snooping by looking for the yellow ribbon. Surely it's here and surely it's torn. Constance has several ribbons hanging next to her mirror. None are yellow.

You keep searching the room and pass by the trash can. There, at the bottom, is a single yellow ribbon. One end is jagged and torn.

"Bingo."

But when you make your way to the closet and discover a sea of yellow items, you wonder if you should abandon this particular line of searching.

You slump back into Constance's desk chair. Who had the motive to attack you? "Think, Pearl, think!" You go down the list . . .

Turn to the next page.

"Constance hated me, that's a no-brainer. Sawyer is an obvious choice—it's his knife that did me in." You spot a red jar of paint on Constance's desk and without thinking you begin trying to move it with your mind. "Then there's Lucy. She is accident-prone and always in a sour mood." You have seen her magnetism make multiple metal projectiles fly across a room. She doesn't have motive, but if it was an accident, she'd be one to keep the secret. "Then there's—" The jar of paint teeters, falls off the desk, and spills onto the floor. Oops.

You shake your head. "It could be anyone!"

Jack and Saelor are pranksters—they could have somehow accidentally dropped a dagger onto your head.

Sal climbs things and could have knocked something over on top of you.

It could be the Headmistress's cat.

Or Mr. Fitzherbert.

Or even . . . Elwyn? Your best friend. Could he have had a time-traveling accident that took you down in the process?

"No. Stop spiraling, Pearl," you console yourself. "Focus on the obvious culprits, Constance and—"

Suddenly you hear voices in the hall. You move toward the door and press your ear against it to hear better.

"We need to meet," you hear Sawyer say.

"Shhh," Lucy says back. "Ten minutes. Don't let anyone see you."

What could they possibly be meeting about in secret? Should you follow them? Then again, you're sure Constance knows something: you get the sense that every time you're around her, it's like she knows you're there.

If you stay in Constance's room, turn to page 128.

If you follow Sawyer and Lucy, turn to page 133.

Bird's-Eye View

You search for Sal in their dorm room, but when you don't find them there, you know exactly where to go. The north turret. It's the tallest, after the Headmistress's office, of course.

As you suspected, Sal is opening the window. They're the only one allowed to venture up here as part of their practice in mastering their gifts.

Sal's specialty is climbing and balancing exceptionally high. As a young child, they would scale the kitchen cabinets in their home, climb to the tops of trees, and sneak out their window to get to the roof. It got to the point where Sal's parents had to put alarms all over the house to warn them their child might be in danger.

But Sal never fell.

Finally, their parents gave up on confining Sal and allowed them to explore their gifts. But Sal kept receiving citations for scaling buildings and bridges and causing accidents by onlookers. They enrolled at Old Willow to be able to master their gift without potentially creating a ten-car pileup.

You peek out the window and instantly regret it. You still very much have the same fear of heights you had in life. Which is not ideal.

Sal ties their wavy hair up into a top bun and opens the window for their afternoon climb.

You reluctantly hook your arm around theirs. If they notice, it's not obvious. You cling to them like your life depends on it and even manage to crack a smile at the irony of it.

"This is good . . . It'll be fine . . . Totally worth it to get a good look at everything . . ." You feel a little better after the self-pep talk, but not for long.

Linked to Sal, you climb up the outside of the turret, along the slanted roof, and up the tall weather vane.

The ornament at the top of the weather vane is a black cat. Of course it is. You never noticed that before.

Just when you've talked yourself into fully opening your eyes, you are pulled from Sal!

Turn to page 78.

78

Against your will, some unknown force rips you from your friend, your safety net, forces you through the sky at a terribly fast pace, and plants you right in the center of the hedge maze far below.

There you are stuck.

The hedge maze used to be your favorite place. Now it's a prison.

Every time you get close to finding the exit, you're whisked back to the middle!

You spend eternity stuck in this torturous loop.

Worse, you swear the cat on the weather vane mocks you.

The End

Creepy Crawlies

Saelor Valor was born in a small cottage in the woods to parents who farmed truffles and rare mushroom varieties. Her gifts were first realized after her mother complained of invasive insects preying on their precious truffles.

Saelor simply told her mother, "Ask them to stay away!" It was cute and her mother had a good laugh over her precocious daughter's suggestion.

But the insects suddenly did stay away.

The older Saelor got, though, the more she experimented with this gift. She could convince butterflies to decorate her bedroom, ants to swarm and kill the poison ivy, and wasps to sting the annoying cicadas.

She also realized she could use her gifts to her advantage.

To torture Tommy Wright, for instance.

Tommy Wright who once left Saelor at the bottom of a muddy ravine after promising her a candied apple for daring to venture down in the first place. Tommy Wright who pulled her signature beet-dyed pink hair and abandoned her during games of hide-and-seek and tricked her into eating an actual mud pie. Oh yes, Tommy Wright, the boy who awoke to a squad of scorpions in his bed for five days in a row. Tommy Wright who would find maggots in his morning oatmeal. Tommy Wright whose bathwater was inexplicably swarming with water beetles. Yes, *that* Tommy Wright.

Saelor considered the insects her friends, and she truly did learn to care for them. So, when it came time for her class to do dissections, she refused. But her teachers forced her hand. In response, she set the hundreds of slimy crawlers free. Saelor tried to convince the worms to dissect her teachers instead, but they lacked opposable thumbs.

The worms did, however, tie the teachers to chairs and gag their mouths.

This stunt is what finally sent Saelor to Old Willow.

Turn to the next page.

80

You enter Saelor's room to find her sitting on her bed. You weren't extremely close friends, but she seems upset, the way she's nudging a beetle across her comforter.

"Hey, Saelor," you say. You don't expect a response but figure you'll try anyway.

You're not exactly sure how to "borrow" someone's gifts, but it kind of worked with Lucy, though you didn't have much say in it. Nevertheless, you crouch down next to Saelor and concentrate on the beetle. Similar to how you move things with your mind, you picture the beetle turning in a circle but also concentrate on Saelor and try to imagine what she's thinking about.

To your surprise, a flurry of images flashes inside your mind, but they're not your images, they're Saelor's. And they're easy to discern from your own because hers are all blurry and tinted pink. If ever you were connecting to Saelor, it's now. Again, you picture the beetle spinning in a circle.

Slowly the black shiny thing begins turning to its right. And it keeps going. Faster and faster and faster until it is now only a blur!

"Stop!" Saelor commands, and the beetle halts. She's definitely the boss here. Saelor glances around the room as if confused but doesn't seem any the wiser. Scooping the black beetle up, she drops him into a jar next to the window.

"Okay . . . this could work," you say.

Go on to the next page.

Constance's dorm room is right across the hall.

You slip in by slowly sliding through where the door is open a crack. You enter to find Constance sitting in a chair reading under a lamp. She glances up directly at the door. At you.

"Constance?" you whisper. "I know you can see me."

She returns to her book.

You run up to her. "Boo!" you scream. She doesn't flinch.

"Fine. I've given you several chances. You asked for this."

You lean so you can see Saelor through the crack in Constance's door. You tap into her mind—into her gift.

Spiders are Constance's greatest fear.

You imagine a hundred spiders marching their way down the hall and under the door to Constance's room.

Turn to the next page.

Patiently you wait for them to appear.

You wait . . .

And wait . . .

You're about to abandon ship when eight brown brittle legs skitter under the door. More follow.

It's not a hundred spiders, but it's enough to spook Constance.

You persuade them to climb up the legs of her chair. Then up the wooden arms. Once Constance's chair is made of spiders, you command them to jump onto her book.

Constance screams and jumps out of her chair, sending several spiders flying your way.

You lose your concentration. The spiders scatter.

Constance walks to her door, then locks it shut. You've finally shaken her!

Glancing around the room, you spot a jar of red paint. It takes several tries, but you manage to push it off the shelf so it falls and shatters. There's also a red ribbon hanging next to the mirror. You mean to send it flying, but instead shove her red leather desk chair three inches to the right.

"Stop it, Pearl!" Constance shouts.

Excellent.

"I knew it! I knew you could see me!" But she doesn't respond and she's not looking directly at you. She's actually looking at her dresser to your left.

She rolls her eyes. "No, I can't see you."

How then?

Again, Constance sets her eyes on her dresser. And it hits you. She *can't* see you. But she does know your every move. Constance's gift is communicating with inanimate objects. She's probably known what you've been up to this whole time.

"Mother of Frankenstein," you say.

Now what?

You're having luck with tapping into your friends' gifts, but would it work on your enemy? If you can communicate with inanimate objects, you can communicate directly with Constance.

You could also bypass all that trouble and haunt her into admitting she knows something about your death.

If you try to use Constance's gifts against her, turn to page 137.

If you haunt Constance, turn to page 140.

Hedge Maze Trap

The Headmistress slowly walks down the hall until she's at the bottom of the back staircase that leads to her office up in the highest turret. But instead of going up, she glances over her shoulder, sees no one is around, and quickly leaves through the side door.

It happens so quickly, you almost get the door slammed in your ghost face, but you make it out just in time.

You are granted a fraction of a second to see the Headmistress disappear around the garden fence before you are picked up by an unseen force. The force throws you into the air and whisks you to the hedge maze.

Of course, you know the hedge maze backward and forward, but you've never been randomly dropped inside it before. You're completely disoriented.

To gain your bearings, you climb the tallest hedge and spot the nearest exit.

But . . .

"What the creeps?" you say.

Go on to the next page.

As many times as you've explored every inch of this maze, you've never once noticed the dark red flowers now growing in one spot—a dead end.

The sight of the flowers triggers a memory.

You haven't seen the flowers in the *maze* before, but you *have* seen them. Yesterday. In the Headmistress's office. What had you been doing in there? You can't recall, but you know the same flowers were floating in a jar of fluid locked in one of her drawers. You weren't supposed to see them.

But the memory stops there.

Could they have had something to do with your death?

You'll never know.

Every time you find your way out of the maze you hit an invisible barrier that returns you back to where you started.

You're stuck in the maze but will work to figure out what in the world the Headmistress is using those flowers for even if it . . . kills you.

The End

Someone Call the Police!

Miss Loveland walks at a steady pace down the hall and to the teachers' office. You follow. But when she enters, Mr. Fitzherbert is sitting at the desk. "There is a group of severely distraught students in the parlor awaiting the counselor, who is delayed. You should sit with them, Miss Loveland," he says.

"All right, but I need to call the police first." Miss Loveland grabs for the phone, but Mr. Fitzherbert pushes it aside.

"No need, the Headmistress has already made the call."

She hesitates but takes a step back. "Very well." And she turns to leave.

"Miss Loveland, wait!" you call after her. "Call the police!"

She walks out the door.

Something's fishy—you do not trust Mr. Fitzherbert at all. You move closer to see what you can find out from him when he stands and quickly leaves.

"Great. I guess *I'm* calling the police."

You obviously can't trust any of the adults in the school to handle things. None of them seem overly concerned that you've died mysteriously, save Miss Loveland, but she's not catching on quickly enough.

Using your anger over the incompetent adults around you, you manage to push the phone receiver over and press the emergency button.

When you put your ear to the phone, it's dead.

"Hmm . . . weird." But maybe this phone is out. No one uses the phones much at all here in this remote old school.

You move to the kitchen—the phone there is red, which will hopefully prove helpful.

This time you use your gift on the red phone to push the receiver off. After several tries it moves enough for you to put your ear up to it. Also dead. One dead phone is annoying. Two? Intentional.

Turn to the next page.

"Someone cut the stinking line!" you say. "And if the phones are dead, the Headmistress obviously didn't call the police. Mr. Fitzherbert, you no-good, lying . . ." You continue calling Mr. Fitzherbert names that would get you into trouble if anyone could hear you, and follow the phone wire along the wall and out of the kitchen. From there, the wire enters the wall up near the ceiling.

The only other phone you're aware of, besides the one in the Headmistress's office, is in the infirmary upstairs. Quickly, you scale the stairs, and in the small library next door to the infirmary, you find the wire. It's way up in the very top corner of the vaulted ceiling and is jaggedly cut in half.

"How the creeps did someone get up there?"

Well, Sal is known for scaling great heights, and this would be nothing for them. But there's not much to hold onto. Bookshelves, though they're extremely narrow.

Sawyer could easily throw a knife or shoot an arrow and slice the cord. Probably with his eyes closed.

And it's possible Saelor sent an insect up there to chomp through the wire.

There's also Benedict the cat, who has been known to destroy a wire or two, among other things.

Great.

Go on to the next page.

You haven't narrowed anything down—you've only expanded your list of possible suspects!

There's no dagger to be found.

And you can't even tell anyone!

It would seem you're on your own. No one is going to solve this murder but you. "Think, Pearl, think!" you say to yourself. What are some things they do in murder mysteries? You look around the room to spur your memories and your eyes settle on a bookshelf. "That's it! Murderers always return to the scene of the crime."

But it would be nice to have some help. A bit of backup. There's an ancient radio in the creepy basement left from before there was a telephone line at the old boarding school. It's kept in working order for emergencies. Now might be the time to test it out.

If you return to the scene of the crime, turn to page 144.

If you use the radio, turn to page 148.

Doors to Nowhere

Rumor has it, the original couple who owned the home that became the school hoped to fill it with children, but sadly never did. Sadder still, the woman died at a young age, leaving her husband to grieve in the huge empty house. In his grief and boredom, and with more money than he knew what to do with, he started collecting cursed and haunted items. Some were highly valuable and questionably acquired. To keep them safe, he created countless secret hiding places in the home. Some were decoys, others are rumored to have never been discovered to this day.

The one in the library is well known, but students are not allowed to access it.

That won't stop you.

The switch matches the wall and is partially hidden by a bookcase. Using your newfound ability to make contact with things by tapping into your emotions, you try to move the switch to trigger the door. You're surprised to realize it's much easier than turning a doorknob. After a few tries, you flip the switch.

Go on to the next page.

The hidden door slides open. Everyone gasps at the noise and the door opening seemingly on its own. You quickly slip inside the passageway—it leads to the small library downstairs.

"Students," Miss Loveland says, her voice shaky. "Please, everyone to your dorm rooms at once." On her way out, Miss Loveland flips the switch and the door slides closed.

"Miss Loveland, no!" you shout.

You panic, then remember—thank goodness—there's another door.

It's completely dark, but you carefully feel along the jagged stone walls as you take the short staircase down to what you assume is the first floor. When you finally get to the door at the bottom, you search for the switch.

Turn to the next page.

92

There is no switch but there is a very large metal lever. You can't see it, but you imagine it's old, rusty, and heavy. At first you simply try to push the lever up. Then you try to push it down. Then to the side. Then to the other side.

It will not budge.

You change tactics and put all your anger into it. The lever doesn't so much as shift.

"Come on!"

You try again. And again. You scream and cry and try to bust through the door or the walls, even the ceiling and floor.

This goes on for days . . . weeks . . . maybe months. Until time has no meaning.

You live out your ghostly days waiting for someone to enter the old passageway.

But it appears to be stuck on both ends.

The End

Pastries

It's a tricky, tight squeeze, but you manage to push your way out the cat door. Luckily for you, Benedict isn't a small cat. It's much easier than trying to open a door. And the Headmistress's darling feline has many of his own entrances throughout the house.

Your plan was to make your way to the hedge maze to think, but when you consider it further you decide it might not be the most productive use of your time. Instead, you decide to focus on a student, and Lucy was the last one you saw leave the library.

You walk in the direction you saw her going and consider Lucy's possible involvement in your death. She does have magnetism. The dagger could have stuck to her back at the library and she might not even notice. Or maybe she intentionally stuck it to herself to hide evidence.

You find Lucy—and bonus, Constance—both in the kitchen having a snack. They're eating the blackberry Danishes the cook had prepared for afternoon tea. It's strange that they're here since students were told to go directly to their dorm rooms. Who could so casually grab a snack at a time like this? You intend to find out.

You see a couple of options before you. Leaving a message in blackberry Danish filling might be effective. Or, since Constance's gift is to speak with inanimate objects, you could threaten that table that if it doesn't pass along a message, you will lie on top of it forever.

If you leave a message in blackberry filling,
turn to page 149.

If you threaten the table, turn to page 150.

Secrets Revealed

Elwyn bolts out the door, but quick thinking, action, and the fact that you're already not too far behind him keeps you close on his heels.

You don't even get to celebrate finally escaping the library, you're so focused on catching up with him. As you speed-walk to keep up, you also use any emotion and energy you can muster to make contact with things. You toss, push, shove, and kick anything and everything in your path until Elwyn is so freaked out he breaks into a run.

Running after him, you do feel bad. You're torturing your bereaved best friend!

"I'm sorry, Elwyn, but it's for the greater good!" you shout, giving him a couple of sharp pokes. Nothing seems to be getting through his thick skull except that he's really creeped out. He doesn't seem to have any idea it's you or could be you. What he thinks it is, you have no idea.

Probably some student's untapped gifts. It's happened before. Messing with these things without knowing their full extent can be dangerous.

Go on to the next page.

When Elwyn finally gets to his room he flies through the door and slams it shut. You manage to squeeze in just in time.

He locks the door for good measure. Little does he know what he's hiding from is standing right next to him.

Time to change tactics.

You begin searching his room for something that will without doubt alert him it's you, Pearl, his best friend, who's messing with him.

You refuse to give up until you try one more thing. But it's got to be good.

Turn to the next page.

98

You remember something.

Elwyn keeps a stuffed toy lizard under his bed that he sleeps with. He's had it as long as he can remember and on the nights he has trouble sleeping, he digs it out. He's claimed only you know about it, and you believe him.

You force yourself to crawl under the bed. When you see the lizard, you work on gripping it as tight as you can. Then, using your last energy reserves, you yank the toy out and fling it into the middle of the room.

"P-Pearl?" Elwyn speaks in a near whisper. He's staring wide-eyed at the toy.

"Finally," you say through a yawn, crawling next to where the lizard landed, all sad, legs splayed. You pick one leg up, hoping Elwyn will understand it means yes.

He gasps but seems to understand because he asks you another question.

"Are you—I mean, did you . . . die?"

Right leg for yes.

Elwyn sort of falls onto his bed. "Do you know what happened?"

Left leg for no.

"Okay . . ." Now he stands and begins pacing. "So, are you a ghost?"

First you lift the right leg because you're pretty sure that's what you are. But then you also lift the left leg because who really knows?

As Elwyn tries to come up with another question, your eyes grow heavy. Moving the lizard has taken all your energy and you must sleep.

"Pearl?"

Come on, Pearl, snap out of it! You stand up, start pacing the room. This is not the time to nap, you have a murder to solve!

Now that Elwyn knows you're here, you can use his non-ghost advantages to help solve your murder. And as a non-ghost, he can search bedrooms much more efficiently than you. And you make a great lookout.

But maybe you shouldn't rush into this. You and Elwyn still need to figure out how to communicate with one another.

If you have Elwyn search students' bedrooms, turn to page 152.

If you and Elwyn practice communicating, turn to page 158.

The Tomb

"Students to your dorms. Now!" the Headmistress announces.

Everyone—adults included—seems pretty creeped out and they all scatter and leave.

You're alone.

Well, sort of.

With a deep breath, you approach your body. Staring down at yourself is strange and dizzying. But you push your discomfort aside and search the area that surrounds the other you. You look under the chair again, on the table, in the nearby bookshelves, but nothing is out of place. Nothing stands out.

You return to your body and try to roll yourself over to get a better look at where you believe the dagger was used to knock you over the head.

But just as you're fighting to lift your head up off the floor, the Headmisteress's assistant, Mr. Fitzherbert bursts through the door pushing a rickety metal rolling table. The man walks with a hunch, wears a black suit, and has long graying stringy hair. He certainly looks the part of an undertaker.

Go on to the next page.

Following close behind is a surprisingly composed Headmistress. Her hair is fixed—smoothed back into her usual tight bun—and she's changed out of the yellow top she had on into a red floral one. She watches as Mr. Fitzherbert lifts your body and sets you on the table.

Benedict curls himself around her feet and she lifts him like a large, furry baby into her arms. He mews and side-eyes you.

"You know what to do, Fitzherbert," she says gravely, motioning him to leave.

He doesn't hesitate in strapping your body to the table. Nor does he mention the police or a doctor.

You quickly hop on the table along with . . . yourself.

Turn to the next page.

102

Mr. Fitzherbert rolls your body through a long tunnel you've never seen before that leads to the old, damp basement. Once at the bottom of the tunnel, you are rolled through a door. Above it, carved in stone, reads: HIC SUNT INFELICES.

"Here rest the unfortunate," you translate. Everyone at Old Willow takes Latin.

Mr. Fitzherbert releases your body from the table and places it inside a stone tomb. He leaves and the door slams and locks with finality.

You take a small tour of the tomb and realize it is filled with other students, those who somehow met your same fate.

Slowly, some of their ghosts come out of hiding.

You're trapped for eternity, but at least you're not alone.

The End

Redo

Elwyn starts toward the library and you follow close behind. But he slows to a stop, and you nearly run into him . . . or pass through him.

"Pearl," he says, "you're here, right?"

You give him a soft poke in response.

Elwyn takes a deep breath and nods. He takes off running again. This time you stay by his side.

You both enter the library to find the Headmistress inside. Her back faces you and she's leaning over, cleaning something with her apron.

Go on to the next page.

You move in to see what she's up to, but she turns around and sees Elwyn. She gasps and drops the dagger, which she quickly kicks under the chair.

"Let's get out of here, Pearl!" Elwyn shouts, running back out of the library.

You manage to grab Elwyn's arm just as he time travels to escape. But instead of arriving in another location in the school, you end up in the hedge maze.

You have no idea if you traveled to the present or the past.

You're laughing as you glance over at Elwyn, because of course he's stuck you smack dab in another predicament before you've figured out the last one.

He smiles back at you. Tears in his eyes, he says, "Pearl?"

Turn to the next page.

106

It's strange, as if he *sees* you. Can he? Elwyn has explained that when he time travels some things aren't the same: he can go places he normally couldn't or he can hear and see things more clearly than usual. Maybe he *can* see you? Or maybe the ghost rules don't apply in time travel reality?

When you glance down at your body, you're still misty and sheer. But it's foggy in the hedge maze. He must see your outlined form.

You wave. He waves back. It's exciting but also sad. He steps closer, attempts to touch your shoulder, but his hand only falls. You shrug and try to give him a smile.

"I'll follow you this time," he says.

You nod and motion for him to come along. On your way, though, you stop dead with the triggering of a memory: you pass by a large bush of dark red flowers you've never seen before.

"Those are new," you say.

Elwyn doesn't hear you, but he also says, "I don't remember these." Elwyn plucks one off the bush and smells it. He makes a disgusted face. "They smell like turpentine."

And yet another memory hits you: you have seen these flowers before. Floating in a jar in the Headmistress's office. Yesterday. The jar was closed, but there was a distinctively sour chemical stink of turpentine.

Go on to the next page.

This gives you an idea. You have the perfect opportunity to break into the Headmistress's office, and you and Elwyn can search the space for clues.

But time could be running out. With Elwyn's gift as unpredictable as it is, going back into the school increases your risk of seeing either of your other selves, which is Elwyn's top "Time Traveling Never Ever."

"If you encounter yourself, you end up Lost in Time," he had gravely explained several times.

Now that you've seen the Headmistress with the murder weapon, maybe you should convince Elwyn to try to travel back to the present immediately. That way, you can work on recruiting other students to help find the evidence you need to take her down.

If you and Elwyn break into the Headmistress's office, turn to page 164.

If you travel back to the present to recruit your fellow students and prove the Headmistress is guilty, turn to page 170.

The Space-Time Continuum . . . Or Something

The first place you're going to search is your dorm room. If you are still alive, someone has to warn you about what's going to happen!

You just hope you're not too late.

As you take off in the opposite direction from Elwyn, he skids to a stop. "Pearl?" he says, his back to you. "That's you, right?" Lacking other options, you knock three times on the wall. Elwyn turns and smiles. "Be careful, Pearl. Remember, you can't have any contact with your other self."

You knock to let him know you hear.

He takes off again, shouting, "I mean it, look alive, Pearl!" which you would find funny under different circumstances. None of his space-time continuum stuff matters. You're a ghost—your other self can't see you!

You burst through your bedroom door just in time to see yourself standing up from your desk to leave. It must be close to dinnertime based on the light coming in through the window.

When the past you turns around and faces the ghost you, several things happen in quick succession.

The past you gasps and drops the watch she was buckling to her wrist.

"Can you see me?" you say, equally shocked.

But you don't get to hear a reply because the brightest white light engulfs the space. There is nothing but white. No shadows. No textures. Just white.

That is, until an indeterminate amount of time passes and your vision begins to heal. Your surroundings slowly come into focus.

"Oh no," you say, your voice echoing like a whisper into what must be eternity.

You are surrounded by nothing at all and infinite space. You can feel the ground under your feet but cannot truly see it because everything, all matter, is the same.

Turn to the next page.

110

"Lost in time," you muse into eternity.

You've heard Elwyn go on and on about this so many times you stopped listening a while ago. Now you're wishing you hadn't.

"It's the space-time continuum, Pearl. You just don't mess with time and space!"

You do recall snorting in laugher, angering your best friend and then forcing yourself to be serious. "Well, what happens if you run into yourself during another time?"

"Purgatory. Destitution. Nothingness."

"What? Stop, Elwyn, be serious."

And the way he looked at you, you knew he was serious. At least for that moment.

"Lost in time. You'd be lost in time," he said.

You decided not to press anymore. Now you understand why. Because of your impulsiveness and lack of listening and taking your best friend seriously, you are bound to the abyss of eternity for the rest of time.

Selfishly, you hope Elwyn gets himself lost in time too so at least you won't have to be alone for eternity.

The End

More Ghost Rules

When you catch up with Constance, she's in a less-trafficked hallway. She's stopped in front of an old painting. After looking over her shoulder, making sure she's alone, Constance slides the painting over to reveal a door behind it.

There are several secret passageways in the old school. It was originally a large family home, then a home for wayward children. Supposedly it also served as a temporary jail and hospital for a short while.

Constance opens the door and climbs through the opening. You follow before she closes the door and slides a lever overhead which you assume puts the painting back in place. She flips a switch and dim, flickering lights illuminate a stone tunnel before you. It slopes into a sharp decline.

As you continue, you can tell Constance is using her gift to communicate with nearly every inanimate object she passes. Doors open right up for her. The stairs seem to shift. Lanterns illuminate. It's almost as if the objects are showing her the way.

A final passageway leads to an underground river.

Turn to the next page.

You had no idea water ran underneath the old mansion, but you're also not surprised. This massive old home has loads of secrets hiding in the cracks and crevices and apparently also in the spaces beneath it.

Constance stops at a small boat that bobs against the stone siding with the gentle current. She steps in and you don't hesitate to follow. The rope holding the boat in place unties itself and you are afloat, gliding down the river to who knows where. But you intend to find out.

The current pulling the boat intensifies. The faster you flow, the more you feel the need to grip the sides.

"I know you're here, by the way." Constance looks over her shoulder directly at you. *"Pearl."*

The sudden acknowledgment of your existence startles you so much you stand up, wobble, then fall headfirst out of the boat.

You are immediately swept away by the current.

The last thing you hear is Constance shouting, "I was trying to help you, stupid!"

Ghost rule: Ghosts can't swim.

The End

Help! Police!

You rush out of the common room and down the stairs to find a surprisingly composed Headmistress making her way to the door. When she opens it, two policemen greet her. You try everything you can to get their attention, but nothing works. You're just as invisible to them as you are to everyone else.

Except Benedict, apparently. Great help that is.

"What's this?" the Headmistress says.

"We received a call from a student, ma'am" one of the policemen says. "Elwyn Spruce? Possible death?"

The Headmistress pauses. If she's surprised by this revelation, it doesn't show. "Oh my," she says. "I was afraid of this."

The police officer cocks an eyebrow.

"It's the children, you see. They've gone much too far this time."

"How so?" he asks.

"It's the pranks! So many pranks! They plague me. Torture me."

What a hack.

"And now? Oh, I'm just so very embarrassed, now they've wasted your time as well." She puts her head in her hands in what feels like an audition for her Broadway debut. When she looks up, she motions inside. "Can I offer you a cup of tea? It's the least I can do."

"No . . . no, thank you, we're fine." He glances past her and into the school's grand entrance. "We'll be going now."

"Alright. My sincerest apologies. The children in question are being punished as I speak."

He tips his hat and the two of them leave.

The Headmistress closes the massive wooden doors and locks the three locks. She turns and smiles. Wait, no, it's not really a smile, it's more of a smirk.

"Mr. Fitzherbert?" she singsongs.

"Ma'am?" Fitzherbert appears from the shadows like a creep.

"Fetch me Elwyn Spruce," she says, emphasizing every syllable. "Now!" The word echoes through the grand entry hall as spittle sprays in Mr. Fitzherbert's face. He takes off up the grand staircase.

The Headmistress smooths her salt-and-pepper hair and then calls for Benedict, who obediently materializes through the cat door from the parlor.

Elwyn. He's now put a big target on his back. His life could be in danger! With haste, you follow Mr. Fitzherbert.

You must figure out who's responsible for your death, fast, before the killer strikes again. And before the victim is your best friend. You need to find a way to warn Elwyn. But as you're following Mr. Fitzherbert, you pass the common room and catch Sawyer sitting alone in the dim light, staring at his knife case, at the empty spot with the missing dagger.

Strange. Suspicious.

And then there's the scene you just witnessed between the police, the Headmistress, and Mr. Fitzherbert. The Headmistress was quick to lie about pranksters calling the police. Was that to avoid controversy for the school, or is she hiding something?

Again, strange. Suspicious.

Zeroing in on the killer before they strike again is priority number one. Something in your gut is steering you back toward Sawyer.

Turn to page 117.

Daggers

You take advantage of Sawyer being in the common area and search his room.

Of course, he can't see you anyway, but if you decide to try to move something or push a door open, it'll be much less risky if you're alone.

Unsurprisingly, Sawyer's room is spotless and orderly. But there's not a dagger to be found. Even the ones he keeps locked in a glass case are gone.

The only weapons you find are arrows and darts, neither of which are to blame for your current state.

You decide to look at every suspect's bedroom.

You know the Headmistress headed to her office. Even though it's not particularly convenient, you decide to search her room next. You take one of the back stairways to save some time.

The Headmistress's room is all reds and velvets and dark cherry wood. Unlike her office, her bedroom is stark: bed, chest, dressing table, bookshelves. You look everywhere and don't find anything suspicious. Well, other than a few questionable romance novels.

Next is Lucy's room. In complete contrast to Sawyer's room, Lucy's is chaos. Metal objects are bolted to the walls, clothes and papers and books are strewn about, and various small metal odds and ends litter the floor.

Until . . . there, in an open chest, you find not one, not two, but all of Sawyer's daggers. This isn't a simple case of magnetism. And no way would Lucy ever keep knives in her room, because she would be the most in danger! Also, Lucy couldn't kill a fly (not on purpose). Sure, she *could* kill someone—even you—on accident, but never intentionally.

Without warning, Lucy enters the room. She was supposed to be gone longer! You're instantly pulled to her. Something about her magnetism is causing you to be stuck to her like a paper clip.

"The daggers, Lucy, watch out!" But of course, she can't hear you.

Thankfully, they're in the chest and Lucy is far enough away that they've not gone flying. Yet.

Turn to the next page.

118

Still stuck to her, you kick and swing and knock over every item you can. Unfortunately, this also sends a few small metal objects—hair clips, jewelry, aluminum candy wrappers—flying toward Lucy, but you suppose she's used to it by now.

She's more confused by what's making the things go flying than by what's sticking to her. She knows something is going on because she quickly takes a piece of paper and pen and writes "yes" and "no" and then spells out the alphabet. She sets a wooden bracelet down for you to use.

Quickly, you push the bracelet around and spell out "knives" and "chest." She gets it immediately and gasps, glancing at her storage chest. She scoots away from it.

Something occurs to you. It's now glaringly obvious that she had no idea the daggers were in her room. Could someone be trying to frame Lucy?

Through the makeshift Ouija board, you ask her about Sawyer, if he could be framing her for your death. But she claims they were together the night of your death, so it would seem someone is trying to frame them both.

"Sawyer and I had been stupidly—*stupidly!*—playing around in the library the night of your death. We call the game magnets and arrows." She shakes her head. "Anyway, we were terrified we'd somehow had something to do with your death! But you're saying it was a dagger?"

Go on to the next page.

You place the bracelet over "yes."

The door crashes open and the Headmistress bursts into Lucy's room. She pushes Lucy forward toward the chest of daggers. This both separates you from Lucy and causes all the knives to fly toward her. It's then Lucy does something she's only ever done on accident—she forces out an opposite magnetic current. The knives stop, turn completely around, and fly straight for the Headmistress.

All but two stop in midair, shift, and drop into the chest. The weight of them hitting the bottom makes the lid close shut.

The two that weren't contained catch the shoulders of the Headmistress's jacket and pin her to the wall behind her.

With Lucy standing guard over the Headmistress and her pinned to the wall, you use the homemade Ouija board to interrogate the woman.

You spell out the words "why did you come here," and Lucy reads them out loud. Lucy then adds, "To my room. Why are you here?"

"I don't have to answer to you," the Headmistress says.

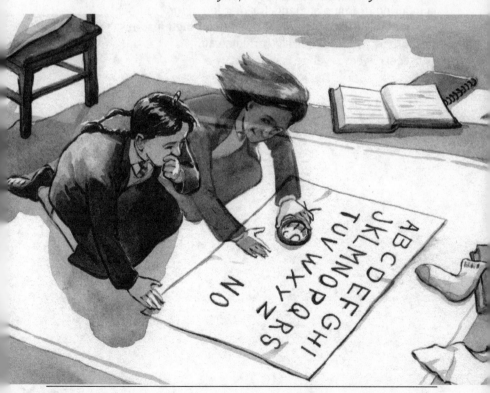

Turn to the next page.

To motivate her to answer, you twist one of the knives holding her captive deeper through her jacket and into the wall.

"I came to catch you with evidence in your room. I received a tip you had something to do with Pearl's death and that you were hiding the murder weapon!"

"L-I-A-R," you spell. Again, Lucy adds, "You know I had nothing to do with that!"

"Then how did Sawyer's daggers end up in *your* bedroom if you didn't use them to kill Pearl?"

"Because I put them here." Mr. Fitzherbert stands in the doorway. "After you told me to."

Seeing the way her eyes darken toward her assistant, her face fills with red rage, you can tell she's been busted, and she knows it.

"I can't be a part of this anymore, ma'am. It's gone too far," he admits.

Mr. Fitzherbert confesses to everything he and the Headmistress have done and then some. Human science experiments, money laundering, framing students for murder, *actual* murder.

Lucy calls the police. They apprehend the Headmistress and Mr. Fitzherbert, who are quickly carted away.

Sweet, sweet revenge is yours.

The End

The Murder Weapon

To break the dagger free, you try to open the drawer with sheer force. Using your anger and emotions, you put all your strength into prying the drawer open, but it's hopeless. The thing doesn't move a centimeter. You search for a key but there are none. Knowing the Headmistress, it's on the master key ring she carries in her skirt pocket.

Looking into the lock, you are able to make out some of the mechanisms. If you could only find a hairpin or paper clip or—

"That's it!" you say.

The Headmistress wears a pin in her hat. One of many hats she keeps on the hat rack next to the door. It takes an excruciating amount of time, but you manage to pull a pin from the Headmistress's hat. It's long, gold, and extremely sharp, with a mother-of-pearl eye.

"This could be a murder weapon," you joke. Sort of.

Using the pin, you work on the lock until you hear the mechanism inside click, and the drawer unlocks.

Turn to the next page.

"Yes!" you shout, yanking the drawer wide open with one motion. You're discovering that when you are experiencing a positive emotion, your ability to make contact with things is even greater.

Ready to try to lift the dagger out of the drawer and carry it far enough to hide it in a new spot, you're instantly distracted by another item. An odd item you didn't expect and a memory you previously did not recall.

The mystery item is a glass jar filled with red liquid and dark red flowers. Under the jar is a list of students.

Images and recollections flood back like quickly rising water, but they're broken and don't make sense.

You recall the Headmistress standing across from you shouting because you found her "notes" and "antidote." The notes are a record that she and her assistant have been testing a sort of medicine—an antidote—on the students from the list. The flowers from the jar are the key ingredient.

Go on to the next page.

You discovered this just yesterday—the day of your murder. The day you broke the founder's red urn and were sent for punishment to the Headmistress's office.

Because the list is underneath the jar, you can't see all of it. You are, however, able to flip it over enough to see some of what's on the back. The heading simply says "Notes." One entry reads like an advertisement:

"This rare, amazing, miraculous antidote cures your child of their destructive tendencies. Embarrassing uncontrollable bouts of telekinesis, time travel, magnetism, and the like are a thing of the past. Don't hesitate another torturous day. Help is here, at the marvelous Old Willow Boarding School for Inflicted Children."

Inflicted?

You read on, now looking over what seems to be a series of notes written in the Headmistress's perfectly slanted script:

"The flowers of the pygmy *hypericus magnimus* tree disrupt neurology, more specifically the electrolysis that occurs in the lesser-known sub-inner lobe of the even lesser-known quantumbellum."

"That doesn't sound good," you say, continuing to read.

"Potential side effects . . ." *Oh no.* "Paralysis, loss of smell and taste, uncontrollable muscle spasms, blackouts, headaches, blackout headaches, intestinal explosion, enlarged vital organs, death."

You flip the paper back over to see about half of the list of students. In one column is their name, in the next a series of check marks or Xs, and in the final column, a place for noted side effects.

Scanning the list, you see Lucy's, Constance's, and Saelor's names. They have only subtle side effects listed. You continue reading. Julius Parker is on the list. He went home weeks ago after suffering a series of horrible headaches. Under "side effects" are the words "massive migraines."

Turn to the next page.

124

Susie McGee is also listed. After her name are several Xs followed by a long list of side effects that includes nonstop indigestion, vomiting, loss of finger (right hand, pointer).

Loss of finger?

Susie McGee also left suddenly, supposedly transferring to another school.

"She's like a mad scientist," you say out loud. You feel sick. "She's a monster."

The dagger sits in the back of the drawer, now only part of the story, and, you fear, a much smaller part than you realized.

"What now, Pearl? What the creeps do you do now?" You tap your fingers on the desk, which feels more like staticky cotton than wood, racking your brain for a plan.

You have the dagger, a list, and notes, as well as the Headmistress's "antidote." But you can't really pick up or move any of it far enough to show it to anyone!

You're going to need help.

And the first step is making contact with your fellow students. But carefully, because you don't know who you can trust.

Elwyn is the obvious choice. He's the only one you're confident wasn't involved. Or, perhaps leaving a message in a public place like the kitchen will scare someone into admitting they know something. It would be a sort of two-for-one scenario: prove you're still there and snuff out a potential culprit.

If you attempt to make contact with Elwyn,
turn to page 174.

If you leave a message in the kitchen,
turn to page 179.

Messages From the Grave

The Headmistress's office is more like a closet of curiosities than a workspace. You realize the only time you've been here was for punishment, and when being punished by the Headmistress, one must stay seated as if one's bum is glued to the chair (by threat of one's bum actually being glued to the chair).

Now that you're able to snoop under the cover of your ghostliness, this space shows a much darker reality. There is a shelf of specimens—plants, insects, animal organs, and several jars labeled "unknown." As you search, you discover a chest. The cellphone chest to be precise! With some precarious positioning of your hands, and using your pent-up ghost frustration as energy, you manage to shift the lid enough so it falls off and to the ground.

The phones are lined up alphabetically, face up. Excellent.

Yours is the fourth one on the fifth row. First you push emotion-fueled energy into the tip of your finger—to do this, you imagine all the pressure and tightness built up in your chest flowing down your arm and to your hand.

Turn to the next page.

It takes a few seconds, but your phone powers on.

"Mother of Frankenstein, only two percent of battery!" You're definitely in the red. You navigate to the "call" screen and hit the emergency button. As soon as someone answers, you end the call. They're required to send someone out to do a safety check and you hope it proves helpful.

With the last bit of your battery life, you text your parents that you love them.

Then—because you can't pass up the opportunity when a perfect prank presents itself—you text Constance, Sawyer, Lucy, and Jack at once. The message simply says, I know what you did and I'm watching! —Pearl. How freaked out will they be when they get their phones back at the end of the year?

Last but not least, you text Elwyn. I'm a ghost and I'm at OW. I miss you, Space Boy. You use your personal nickname for him so he knows it's you.

Your phone dies.

Go on to the next page.

The energy, while released in small bursts, has taken more of a toll than you expected. You push yourself away from the phone trunk, sink to the floor, and fall into a deep sleep.

What feels like days later, you awaken to the sound of harsh loud bangs at the door.

Energy renewed, you rush downstairs to find the police are there. They've actually been there since your call and have been interviewing the students and staff of Old Willow Boarding School.

Your body was recovered—instead of calling the police or hospital, the Headmistress and Mr. Fitzherbert had buried you in the family plot out back, and apparently did it with haste as it wasn't hard for the police to find.

While searching the school and grounds, the police find the bloody dagger in the Headmistress's office, sealing her fate.

She's happy to take Mr. Fitzherbert down with her. Actually, she blames it all on him.

The police don't buy it and they are both taken to jail.

You eventually find several ways to communicate with your friends—writing on the chalkboard, using Constance's old creepy Ouija board, and spelling with different word games.

You also find many ways to scare them too.

Being a ghost isn't so bad.

The End

Keep Your Friends Close and Your Enemies Closer

It's rumored Constance Montgomery was a strange child.

She did not speak a word until she was three and didn't speak in sentences until the age of five. Didn't speak, that is, to other people. She had wonderfully sophisticated conversations with her nightstand though. And her hairbrush was particularly chatty. The stuffed toy elephant she slept next to each night had quite the attitude, but the mirror on her vanity was good at keeping the peace.

Constance ended up at Old Willow after she figured out the inanimate objects could communicate with one another and had a sort of alert system. Constance set up a roadside fortune-telling stand. After using her gift to find out secrets and information about her neighbors, she made a killing "seeing into the future" while swindling her neighbors out of money.

Her parents were not pleased.

Go on to the next page.

A week later, she moved into the Old Willow Boarding School.

"What in the—" Constance enters the room and sees that the red jar of paint has spilled onto the floor. She looks around as if hoping to catch someone in her room, but of course, no one is there. Still, she seems to look right at you.

She glances at the clock and then the bed and then right at you.

And it hits you. Constance is communicating with the items in her room, all around the school. How did you not realize it sooner?

"I know you know I'm here," you say. "Lamp—tell her I know she knows I'm here! Desk—same thing! Carpet—you too!" You keep calling out items and demanding they deliver your message to Constance until finally—

"Enough! Please—stop! I can't take you all talking at once!" Constance covers her ears with her hands and slumps down onto the bed. You take a tentative step toward her. "I know you're here, Pearl. I've known for a while."

You stop. Even though you assumed it was so, hearing her say it out loud catches you by surprise. The fact that someone finally knows you are present is a shock.

Turn to the next page.

130

"Lamp—tell her I hear her," you say, perhaps a bit overly excited.

"I know you can hear me, twit. Stop being so demanding. You can talk to them like you talk to people."

"Oh. Sorry." You cautiously move closer to Constance and sit on the chair nearest her bed. "Why did you pretend you didn't know I was here? I mean, I know you hate me, but it feels particularly cruel considering the circumstances. Even for you." You sort of regret the last part but also you don't.

She takes longer to reply this time and seems to be thinking things over. It's possible she regrets acknowledging you at all. But the cat's out of the bag now.

Finally, Constance takes a deep breath and says, "I don't *hate* you. I'm just annoyed by you . . . by your being here at Old Willow. If I'm being honest, I'm mad you took Elwyn from me. Elwyn and I were best friends before you came here, you know."

You start to explain, but she cuts you off.

"I know, I know, it wasn't intentional. It's probably childish of me to still be angry over it. But I am." She crosses her arms over her chest, and you decide it's best to move on.

"Constance, why did you pretend not to know I was still here?"

Constance wipes her eyes with her sleeve and pastes a stern look on her face.

"I don't know. I just didn't want to deal with it. With you."

"That's pretty clear."

She takes a deep breath. "Last night, I'd gone to bed early and my pillow woke me. It's very rude like that sometimes. Anyway, it woke me to alert me you were in trouble." Somehow she glares right at you. "I didn't want to help you. I kind of wish Pillow hadn't said a thing. But I also didn't want you to get hurt or injured or something, so I got up and went to the library."

"Thank you, Constance, I—"

"I'm not finished. And don't thank me—you still ended up dead, stupid." True. "Once in the library, I was talking to the candlestick on the mantel. But its voice is so quiet, I couldn't hear what it was saying. I moved in to get closer, tripped on the carpet, and knocked the heavy thing into the mirror. When I leaned in to check the damage and clean it up, my ribbon caught on the glass.

"That's when the Headmistress entered. I panicked and tossed the broken shard of mirror into the fireplace."

Turn to page 132.

132

"Did you get in trouble for being in the library after hours?"

"Surprisingly, no. The Headmistress just shooed me off to bed." She scoots back in her bed so she's leaning against the headboard, knees pulled up to her chest. "I snuck back down later after my clock woke me. I . . . I was too late." She shakes her head regretfully. "I should have told someone. I should have said something, I know. But I was terrified I'd be blamed, especially with our history. I came back to bed and tried to forget what I'd seen."

It's quiet for several minutes.

Then, at the same time, you and Constance say:

"—Will you help me?"

"—I want to help you."

You share an uncharacteristically pleasant laugh.

"Yes. I'll help you," Constance confirms. "This is what I know so far . . ."

Constance explains that the night you died, she saw Saelor and Jack planning a prank and she heard your name mentioned. They would never intentionally hurt you, but their pranks have been known to go wrong, with sometimes gory consequences. You and Constance discuss tracking down Saelor and Jack to further investigate their possible involvement.

"But that's only two options," you say. "What about other suspects?"

Constance stands and starts pacing. She's mumbling at various objects until she stops and faces several candles. "That's it!" she says. "A séance!"

"I'm sorry, a what?"

"We'll have a séance. It means contacting the dead . . . aside from you, obviously. I dabble. It will scare any students who know anything into spilling the truth. Unless you think we should just focus on Saelor and Jack."

If you track down Saelor and Jack, turn to page 180.

If you have a séance, turn to page 185.

Friends or Foes

You follow Lucy as she makes her way to what is apparently her and Sawyer's secret meeting place. But the closer you get, the more you get the strange feeling you're being pulled along with her.

Before you register what's happening, you *are* pulled right next to her. Much like a magnet.

"What the creeps? Lucy, let go!" you shout. Of course, she can't hear you and, of course, you know she can't let go. It would seem some sort of magnetic reaction is occurring between your ghostly form and Lucy.

You have no control over where you're going and panic sets in. You try to fight it, try to pull yourself away. Then you push yourself into Lucy, hoping some sort of opposite reaction will occur.

It doesn't work and now you're even more stuck!

"Mother of Frankenstein! I like you Lucy, but I do not want to be stuck to you, for eternity!"

As you get closer to the intended destination, you realize you are heading to the greenhouse that lacks much green and doubles as the Old Willow ancestral graveyard.

Old Willow Boarding School used to be Old Willow Manor. It was owned for generations by the Willow family. Rumor has it that the Headmistress inherited it from the founder, who was a direct descendant of the original Willows. The founder was also great-uncle to the Headmistress, who is now the sole living family member. And it is here her ancestors, their pets, and a few notable past headmistresses are buried.

Lucy drags you along to meet Sawyer, who is hiding behind a large spindly statue of a woman weeping. You expect to get to overhear fantastical revelations about your death. How their prank of the year went horribly wrong and how they feel awful and will suffer that guilt the rest of their lives.

Instead, they settle into a betting game called Tidbits that uses cards and marbles. It was banned months ago.

"You've got to be kidding me," you say as you're pulled to the ground by Lucy when she sits.

Turn to the next page.

134

You wait impatiently for them to finish—Lucy wipes the floor with Sawyer. It isn't until they make their way to the door that leads to the main house that you can grab onto a nearby statue for dear life. You put everything you have into your grip as you hug the stone figure.

Finally, as Lucy walks through the doorway and the door closes, you're peeled free. But not fully. When you try to get yourself out of the graveyard, you can't even touch the door. Every time you try, you are shocked with an electric jolt.

You search the grounds in hopes of finding another way out, but what you discover is much more disturbing than being stuck in an old graveyard for eternity.

The cat cemetery.

Benedict Senior, Benedict Junior, and every other Benedict in a long line of Benedicts! The space is set apart by a miniature iron spiked fence and tiny gravestones adorned with carvings of catnip toys, fish, mice skeletons, and angel-winged felines.

"Gross," you say, turning your back on the bizarre sight.

That's when you hear a series of odd noises. The scratching of claws on stone. Several guttural growls. And unnatural meowing.

If you still had the ability to produce goosebumps, you'd have them head to toe. Slowly, you turn on your heel.

Before you, guarding their territory, are what you can only describe as *cat zombies*.

Grotesque creatures they are: limbs half attached, fur matted with blood and goo and who knows what else. Some have bones protruding from their flesh. Others show horribly decaying organs, have intestines and other entrails at their hind paws, foam frothing from their fangs.

Turn to page 136.

136

Briefly, you wonder if they've always been here, and no one's seen them because no one ever visits this place, or if you can only see them because you're dead.

Either way, they appear quite hungry.

You're unsure whether they realize you're a ghost and cannot provide the flesh they crave. But you don't wait around to find out.

You run in the opposite direction, climb a tree, and then upon remembering cats also climb trees, you scale the greenhouse until you're at the topmost roof beam.

With a bird's-eye view, you spot a freshly dug grave. Odd, since most of the plots here are ancient. But when you zero in you realize exactly whose grave it is.

The initials on the modest stone clue you in.

P.M.M.

It's yours.

You've found your eternal resting place. However, you're confident there won't be much resting.

The End

Speaking to Walls. Literally.

Constance's gifts prove much harder to tap into. You try the lamp. Her desk. Her chair. Multiple horse figurines. And finally, all four walls. Nothing speaks back.

It would seem inanimate objects are smarter than insects.

Constance leans back casually in her reading chair. "It won't work," she singsongs.

Something shifts in the energy of the room. The walls feel as if they're closing in on you, like intense air pressure. You instantly get a splitting headache.

"Oh, you've really done it now," Constance says insufferably. "And to think I considered helping you. Not after this, Pearl. You don't mess with other people's gifts!" She gets up and leaves the room.

The situation takes a turn.

You are hit with massive amounts of information and words and emotions, but it's so much that it's all noise. Loud, loud noise. You clap your hands over your ears and take off out of the room. But it doesn't stop.

The booming noise, the physical force of it, pushes you along the hallway, down the back stairs, through the doorway that leads to the long enclosed walkway, and out to the tombs. You're not sure what or who is buried there and you don't intend to find out.

Unfortunately, you will.

Turn to page 139.

The blaring of every inanimate object you pass disorients you and the pushing of air pressure constricts your body. With one final push, you are shoved through the stone walls of a tomb.

The sensation is horrible. It's clear now you couldn't walk through walls and doors yourself because you don't have the strength. It takes a gazillion everyday objects to join forces to make that happen.

The stone is thick and feels like rabbit fur as you burst through it. It's ink black on the other side and you worry if this tomb's current residents mind you trespassing.

You also would rather not meet your new roommates.

"Hello?" you say.

No one answers.

In what you assume to be a final act of "kindness" a small lantern lights, casting the stone tomb in shadows. There are random bones strewn about, but nothing resembling a whole skeleton or person.

You suppose you should accept your fate and rest in this place built for resting. Instead, you use the bones to try to find a way out.

The End

Ghost Things

Constance knows you're there. In fact, she's been getting a play by play of your every move through the inanimate objects she communicates with.

"Constance, what do you know about my death?" You look around at all the items in the room. You know they're telling her what's happening. Still, she continues ignoring you.

You start by flicking a red paper clip from off her desk across the room. In life, you got pretty good at that trick.

She doesn't acknowledge it.

Next you use your frustration to shove the sweater she has slung over her desk chair onto the floor. Then, accessing that same energy, you cause a slew of her hair ribbons to fly off the wall. Still nothing.

How dare she completely ignore you? You're asking for help! And you know she knows something.

Go on to the next page.

"Constance, please. I need help." You walk straight up to her, lean down so you're eye to eye. "I know you know what I'm saying. And I know you know something about the night I was killed!"

She crosses her arms over her chest and looks away.

Anger boils in your chest. You march straight over to her shelf and knock one of her horse figurines off. It shatters into several pieces on the floor.

This seems to spur her to say, "There are other ghosts in the school. You should find them, maybe they can help. I'm told they hang out in the cellars. Follow the tunnel on the right and enter the fourth door." She stands to leave but looks over her shoulder before she does. "I'm also told that ghosts cannot leave the school and if they do a terrible fate befalls them. I'm going outside. I'd suggest you not follow me."

"Fine," you sigh.

Turn to the next page.

You head straight to the cellars, where a series of tunnels greets you. You're not sure if you should trust Constance, but you also aren't sure what else to go on, so you follow her instructions.

You take the tunnel on the right. And then go through the fourth door, which has been left slightly open, allowing you to push through the space.

You enter to find it's dark, damp, and full of old things, like an attic. There are stacks of framed photos, old dolls, furniture, wigs, and various trinkets. You go to touch one of the curiosities—a doll. But before you even make contact, something pulls you back and screams in your ear.

"That's mine!" the voice shrieks, pulling you away from the dolls. When you turn around, you see it's a little girl. Well, the ghost of a little girl.

"Hello," you say, "can you help—"

But countless pairs of hands pull you backward, through the wall, down some stairs, and through a grate in the floor.

Here you meet the other ghosts Constance spoke of, but they seem more like zombies than anything. They don't talk and they don't go anywhere. They just guard you, making sure you don't leave.

It's like you're their new pet.

This was a trap and you fell right in headfirst.

The End

The Scene of the Crime

You enter the scene of the crime: the library.

There are three libraries at Old Willow: the student library, the main library, and the research library. You enter the main library. This one is the largest, most centrally located, and most ornate. It is the original library to what was once Old Willow Manor.

It is now ten in the evening. All students are to be in their dorm rooms by nine, so the school feels empty. The library is dark save the wall sconces and a dying fire. It's as if nothing has changed from this morning when your body was found, but also, everything has.

Slowly, you approach the spot where your body was found by the Headmistress. Only a small stain discolors the carpet as if it's been scrubbed clean. In the name of "placing yourself at the scene of the crime" you lie down in the exact place you were found and in the exact position: on your back, legs and arms bent in unnatural positions.

Lying back, you rest your head on the carpet, close your eyes, and concentrate.

Someone enters.

Go on to the next page.

It's Lucy, and you know she should not be wandering the school. But it becomes obvious she's sleepwalking after she bumps into several pieces of furniture.

You stand up to investigate, but when you do, you're pulled by her magnetic force right to her. As Lucy sleepwalks and you're pulled along, something flies across the room. The sharp object soars straight through what would be your forehead, narrowly missing your left ear.

"Mother of Frankenstein!" you shout.

Lucy keeps walking, unaware.

Leaning in, but not too close, you whisper in her ear, suggesting she go back to bed.

To your surprise, she shakes her head no.

Can she hear you in her half-asleep state? You test it out. "Lucy, it's Pearl. Can you hear me?"

"Pearl," she says. "This way." Apparently she can! But you don't get a chance to be too excited because she quickly walks across the room.

You follow.

She stops abruptly, and in the dim light you see a letter opener sticking out of the wall before her.

Turn to the next page.

"So that's what it was." You look from the letter opener to Lucy. The letter opener must have been on a shelf, and when Lucy got close enough . . .

"Lucy," you whisper in her ear again. "Did you accidentally kill me?"

"No," she answers quietly, still asleep. "I've been worried it was my prank with Sawyer. We'd been playing around with arrows and magnetism." She lowers her voice to a whisper. "I'm so sorry, Pearl, we didn't mean to . . ."

"You didn't do anything, Lucy," you say. "It wasn't you. Not unless you were playing with daggers, not arrows."

"The Headmistress took Sawyer's knives into the library for cleaning," she says in a monotone.

"When?" you ask.

"Yesterday. Just before dinner."

The Headmistress? Of course! She was at the scene of the crime, she found your body, she was within arm's reach when the dagger went missing, and she hasn't called the police.

You're not sure why she would kill you, but it was her, you know it.

Something about this realization seems to set you free. You rise up, up, up, out of the boarding school, and onto the grounds.

You instantly understand you are now able to go wherever you please.

You choose Iceland.

The End

The Dungeon

The creepy cellar extends the width of the school and is the underbelly of the old building. It is referred to as the dungeon by most of the students.

There are rumblings that the school was built on the foundation of an old prison. The worst of the worst were kept in stone and iron cells below the ground. Ruins from the cells and cast-iron bars and stone still remain.

The radio is in the old security office, which is no longer in use. You plug it into the outlet and sparks fly. You flip the switch and begin to call the police. But before you get all the numbers dialed, the radio is pushed off the desk and cracks in half. Smoke seeps up and out of the old thing.

"What the—" you say, turning around toward the door.

To your shock, there are several disheveled kids in old-timey dress staring daggers at you. They don't look happy.

"Hello," you say, "who are you?"

"We are prisoners of the Jail for Wayward Children, miss," they say in unison. It's horrifying.

"I'm so sorry, I just wanted to borrow your radio."

"You will stay here with us. You have been chosen," they recite. "You are our new nanny."

You try to take off but don't get two steps away before the children circle you, wrap you in their arms, and begin chanting "Ring Around the Rosie."

When they get to "We all fall down!" you are pulled to the ground. When you stand up to brush yourself off you see your clothes are now the same Victorian style they wear.

You've been turned into one of them!

You are condemned to the dungeon to babysit a bunch of Victorian prison children forever.

The End

Sticky Fingers

You stick your ghost finger right into the middle of Lucy's blackberry Danish. Then, on the white counter, you write "Pearl is here."

Lucy jumps out of her chair and points at the writing.

"Wait—was that you?" she asks Constance.

"Nope." She doesn't look concerned. "Maybe it was a prank or something."

"Constance, I saw it happen right before my eyes!"

Constance shrugs. She must be playing it off because she doesn't want Lucy to know for some reason.

Lucy wipes the counter clean.

You dip your finger in again. This time you write "Murder."

Lucy takes off running and you follow—finally you're getting through to someone! Lucy is fast; you're several feet behind her.

When she rounds a sharp corner into the common area, you assume she's headed to Sawyer's room—her usual hiding place. Thinking quickly, you take a shortcut through one of Benedict's cat doors.

But you take the wrong one. This one leads to the cat's indoor play area. It's a jungle gym fit for the most spoiled cat ever.

Benedict follows.

You try to get out, but he guards the door.

"Are you kidding me, furball?" you say.

It is not the right thing to say. Benedict leaves but somehow locks the cat door shut.

The room smells of kitty litter and catnip.

This was not the plan.

The End

Tiny Ghost

You are fed up with no one acknowledging you.

"I know you know I'm here!" You glare at Constance. Then you look to the table where the blackberry Danishes are plated.

"Table," you say, addressing the inanimate object, "help me communicate with Constance or I will lie on top of you and scratch my nails into your beautiful surface and never stop!"

Constance's eyes dart to yours, then to the table. The table rattles. It shifts, scraping the floor. Lucy doesn't seem to notice. Constance only smiles expectantly.

"Fine." You pretend you're not freaked out and climb up onto the table, lying across it. "I'm not leaving."

But the table's not finished.

It almost seems angry. You suppose inanimate objects don't like being threatened any more than people do.

The table shakes again beneath you. It slides across the floor and stops in front of the window.

Lucy gasps. "Constance, what's happening?"

Constance stands, goes to the window, and opens it. "Just airing the place out."

The table tips forward and like a catapult, you are flung outside. The force is so great, you fly across the grounds and land in the walled garden.

When you land, you bounce back up and start running, trying to find your way out of the garden and back to the school.

You don't get far.

It seems that once you leave the school, you cannot get back in and you are punished for this infraction in the most bizarre fashion.

Like Alice after she drinks the "Drink Me" potion, you shrink down to the size of an ant!

It is here, trapped by the massive walls of the garden, that you learn to live among the insects and invasive plants. You also need to learn how to stop getting stuck in morning dew.

The End

The Treatments

With Elwyn's help you take turns figuring out when Constance, Lucy, and Sawyer are out of their dorm rooms for decent amounts of time.

Then you snoop.

But, unfortunately, you don't find much of consequence. The only oddities you find in each of their rooms are passes to see the Headmistress for "treatments."

When Elwyn shows you the passes, several memories about the day of your death come flooding back. The problem is, they're jumbled and mixed up and blurry. You can't make sense of them.

Elwyn corners each of your friends and tries to be inconspicuous about getting information. Emphasis on "tries."

With Constance, he attempts casually asking about meeting with the Headmistress. "Have you ever had to meet with her all by yourself? She gives me the creeps sometimes."

To which Constance simply answers, "No."

He tries to tell Sawyer he's also gotten a pass for "treatments," hoping Sawyer will confide in him. But Sawyer only gives Elwyn a strange look and pretends he has no idea what he's talking about.

Really, his only hope is Lucy. But even that he messes up! "Lucy, do you have any acne *treatment* I can borrow?"

"No," she says, confused.

"What about foot fungus *treatment*?"

"Gross." She shakes her head no.

"Dandruff *treatment*?"

"Elwyn, you need to see the nurse."

Go on to the next page.

Elwyn is getting more and more paranoid and is slipping up big time. You worry he's going to shift the target of the killer onto himself if he keeps acting so strangely.

But when you try to delicately broach the subject, it only makes things worse. So much so that's he's thinking about making a school-wide announcement explaining that he's been speaking with your ghost and that the two of you have a list of suspects.

You feel confident this will backfire spectacularly. You're not sure the best way to handle it, but the answer is probably right under your nose. You need to do more sleuthing.

Turn to the next page.

The Biggest, Greatest, Most Epic Prank

To buy yourselves more time to sleuth and gather clues, you and Elwyn decide on a prank. Something that will get most of the students and teachers out of the school. That way you'll have free rein of the place.

And who better to pull a prank than the best pranksters at Old Willow: Jack and Saelor. (This first requires a lecture from Elwyn about how ghosts are real, and how you are one. Jack and Saelor don't seem to take him seriously until you channel your frustration into throwing a blackberry Danish at Jack's face. After that, Jack and Saelor dutifully listen to everything Elwyn has to say.)

You, Elwyn, Saelor, and Jack sit in a circle on the floor of the rarely used second-floor solarium. "I'm thinking explosions, breaking glass, setting the bats from Mr. Smythe's zoology class free," Jack says, pushing his thick-rimmed glasses back up his nose.

"And bugs—so many bugs." It's the only time Saelor's face ever lights up with pure joy.

Elwyn nods. "We'll leave the prank up to you two—you're the experts. We just need as many people as possible to get out of the school so Pearl and I can look around without being caught."

Go on to the next page.

"No problem," Saelor says, twirling a tarantula-sized spider between her thumb and finger.

Jack shudders. "Do you have to do that here?"

Saelor gives him a look that leaves no doubt about her answer.

"Okaaay." Jack puts his arms up in surrender, then looks at Elwyn. "Just leave it to us!"

"Thank you so much!" you say, then realize they can't hear you. Instead, you give both Jack and Saelor a gentle poke.

They both jump and gasp.

"Sorry," Elwyn says, "I should have warned you. Pearl says thank you."

The two pranksters giggle nervously, and you make a mental note to get them back at some point.

Turn to the next page.

156

After giving Saelor and Jack time to prepare, you and Elwyn hide on the third floor in the empty music room.

You know immediately once things start happening. Fireworks. Smoke. Glass shattering. Bats. All of the things Jack promised. Students scream. Adults call for "calm" and "quiet" and "follow the fire escape routes." But the noise isn't quieting down. No one is leaving.

Then the bugs start up. Beetles, roaches, spiders, ladybugs, praying mantises, moths . . . if it exists in bug form, it's crawling around the school.

"Something's wrong!" Elwyn shouts through the noise and smoke.

You give him a poke in agreement.

"Should we go check?"

Poke.

The two of you follow the sounds of pure chaos to the grand hall. There you find students and teachers huddled in corners and under tables. Some try to pry the door open. It's locked or stuck.

You and Elwyn go to the back doors. The scene is the same.

You check the side doors. They're locked too.

You collect the rest of your friends, and you, Elwyn, Saelor, Jack, Sal, Lucy, and Sawyer split up into groups and check every window and door in the humongous mansion.

They're all sealed shut.

Someone has locked you all in amid a bug and bat infestation!

Fireworks continue to detonate because Jack set them up on timers. Gunpowder smoke fills the school. The bugs are crawling on students. The bats are eating the bugs.

Not only are you a ghost, but you're also now a prisoner surrounded by pandemonium.

It's like the end of the world.

The End

158

You and Elwyn have discovered the best way to communicate is by you tapping on a nearby surface. One knock for no, two knocks for yes, three for I don't know.

Elwyn sometimes gets ahead of himself and forgets he has to ask yes or no questions, but you've started giving four knocks for that, which means you need to relocate to his word game for more options.

"Any ideas what we should do next?"

Two knocks.

Then four knocks.

This is where it gets tricky. And where you move things to the word game by his desk.

When you do, it is decided you need to search for your body. What better evidence is there than a body?

Go on to the next page.

You and Elwyn search everywhere you can think of: the dungeony cellar, the cemetery greenhouse that's connected to the school, and every nook and cranny inside the many rooms of the old manor. You want to search the grounds, but every time you get close to a door or window, something in your gut tells you not to go outside.

Elwyn, of course, isn't aware of the intense anxiety and dread consuming your body as he opens the door to the gardens a crack. You stop and knock on the wall as loudly and quickly as you can.

"Pearl?" He pulls his hand away from the knob. "You okay?"

One knock for no.

"What's wrong?"

How in the world can you explain that for no real specific reason you don't want to leave the house? Glancing around the hallway, trying to find something that might help you explain, you notice the door is still open a crack. As quickly as you can, you slam it shut.

"Whoa!" Elwyn shouts. "Okay, you don't want us to go outside?"

Two knocks for yes. Then . . . one knock for no.

He can still go outside, you just don't want to.

Turn to the next page.

160

With a few more questions and knocks, Elwyn gets the message and goes outside to search. But with the grounds being so vast, and some parts quite forested, he comes back with nothing.

You're about to give up when you decide to search the library one last time. Not necessarily for your body, because where in the world would they put it, but for more clues. Something that possibly went unnoticed.

To let Elwyn know, you sort of push him in that direction. It's not his favorite thing, but he's being a good sport about it.

As you pass through the library, you notice something new on the mantel. A deep red urn. You're able to make it shake slightly to alert Elwyn to check it out. But when you do, a flood of memories comes barreling back to you.

Go on to the next page.

You broke the red founder's urn and spilled his ashes. Your punishment was to organize paperwork in the Headmistress's office. You snooped in a drawer and when you saw that the Headmistress was experimenting on students, you were caught, and the Headmistress silenced you. Forever.

"There's ashes," Elwyn says, unaware of the flash of images you just received. "You think they're—"

But before he can finish, you hook your arm around his and give him a good series of pinches, hoping it spurs him to time travel.

It works.

You're squished and squeezed through space and time and end up at the school a good couple of weeks before your death. You and Elwyn are careful not to run into your other selves as you make your way up to Elwyn's room so you can explain everything using the word game.

Turn to page 163.

You give Elwyn the quick rundown using wild abbreviations and thankfully he knows you well enough to understand. You then have Elwyn write notes to both of your other selves, explaining the full situation.

The two of you hide until you see yourselves read the note.

Then you time travel again and Elwyn does it! He travels intentionally and back to the time you came from. Except, instead of his bedroom, you end up in yours.

"Pearl?" Elwyn says as you're still regaining your balance, figuring out where you are.

"Yeah?"

"Pearl!"

"What!" You stare up at him, annoyed. He's standing in front of your mirror, so in the reflection you see the back of his head and your face.

Your face.

"It worked!" You run and jump at him, scooping him up into an enormous hug. "Thank you! Oh my gosh, thank you!"

He shrugs. "It was nothing." And you both laugh to tears.

Your other selves were able to go to the police. The Headmistress and Mr. Fitzherbert are arrested for their experiments.

Miss Loveland becomes the Headmistress.

And you're alive.

ALIVE!

The End

Hauntings

When you and Elwyn push open the door to the Headmistress's office, at first you think it's empty. But no sooner have you sighed in relief than you see her step out from a storage closet.

Busted.

But she doesn't react to Elwyn standing before her in her office. In fact, she's uncharacteristically calm. Slowly, she sits in her chair. She raises an eyebrow at Elwyn and clasps her hands under her chin. "It's about time you showed up."

"I don't like this one bit," you say, dread building up from your stomach. "We need to get out of here."

You tap Elwyn on the shoulder, hoping he senses the urgency behind it, that he understands you're telling him to run!

He takes a tentative step back and the Headmistress shakes her head in disapproval.

Elwyn takes another step and you can tell he's about to turn and take off, but before either of you can react, Mr. Fitzherbert enters the room from behind you. Large syringe in his hand, he injects Elwyn with the same red liquid you saw in the jar in the Headmistress's desk.

Elwyn stumbles, then falls to the floor. Mr. Fitzherbert lifts Elwyn's limp body over his shoulder and leaves, the Headmistress following. You stay right on their heels as they traverse the back hallways and stairwells of the old mansion.

They finally stop when they reach one of the cellar rooms underneath the school. They leave Elwyn on the stone floor and lock him inside.

Go on to the next page.

There's a square hole in the door that is large enough for you to squeeze through but certainly not large enough for Elwyn to use for escape.

You stay next to Elwyn and wait for him to wake up. He's breathing, and so far doesn't seem injured, but as he lies unconscious, he mumbles and trembles as if having lucid nightmares.

Keeping your arm linked with his, in case he spontaneously time travels, you doze in and out of sleep as well. Flashes of memories come to you in your sleep. You remember being alone with the Headmistress in her office; you remember her injecting you with a syringe. The words "This will cure you of that cursed telekinesis!" in the Headmistress's voice are still ringing in your ears when you wake with a start with Elwyn still asleep beside you.

Turn to the next page.

166

The Headmistress is behind this. You don't know how to stop her, but you know you can start by haunting her. All day, every day.

You have no limit on anger, so smashing things, knocking items over, poking her, it's all fair game. She puts up a good fight, but after the ninth consecutive day of this torture, she leaves Old Willow, claiming early retirement.

Mr. Fitzherbert also retires.

They take all copies of the cellar keys with them along with the evidence of their heinous crimes.

You try and try to release Elwyn from the cellar, but the lock is too complicated and you're not able to fully grip items for long periods of time.

It takes days for you to communicate to your classmates that Elwyn is still stuck in the cellar. You're about to give up all hope when finally Lucy, Constance, and Saelor appear.

Go on to the next page.

Lucy uses her magnetism to jumble the mechanics of the lock. But after several attempts, the door is still stuck.

Constance tries to communicate with the old thing. She spends some time trying, but finally she admits, "This door is too old. We do not speak the same language."

You're not sure if she means that literally or figuratively.

Saelor, your last hope, instructs the massive amounts of spiders in the cellar to band together. They might be tiny spindly things, but they are incredibly strong in numbers.

Turn to page 169.

Saelor pulls her hood up over her head and takes a deep breath. She closes her eyes, whispers something, and, like a moving black shadow, the spiders emerge from the corners and crevices of the cellar.

They flow as one inky stream toward the door.

Using the brute force of many, the spiders manage to shift the heavy door, but not near enough for it to budge.

"Let's try another tactic."

Saelor points at three of the smaller spiders and directs them toward the lock. "They might be small, but they're the smartest of the bunch." She smiles.

The three spiders use their needle-thin legs to maneuver the lock until it clicks.

The lock falls to the floor with a loud thud.

Elwyn opens the door.

Yes, your murderer and her creepy accomplice get away. But you know the truth and Elwyn is free.

You'll take it.

The End

The Mission, Should You Choose to Accept

It's got to be the Headmistress. She's the only suspect that makes sense. The memory of those red flowers you saw in the hedge maze nags at you. Something isn't right.

Elwyn holds a meeting. You're by his side, but of course no one can see you. You did, however, go through everything with Elwyn beforehand using the word game on his nightstand. He's written it all down and reads it aloud to Constance, Jack, Sawyer, Sal, Lucy, and Saelor.

"I've been communicating with Pearl," Elwyn starts. Jack makes to get up, thinking it's a joke, but Constance pulls him back down.

"Just listen, dimwit," she says. She does know you're there, doesn't she?

"Anyway, like we suspected, Pearl was murdered. She and I believe it was the Headmistress who did it. We're not sure why yet, but we have enough evidence to at least get the police here and interested." He looks up at them. "But we're going to need your help."

No one says a word.

"Okay. Lucy, Sawyer, and Constance: We need you to go to the Headmistress's office and retrieve some incriminating evidence we believe is there. A bloody dagger—we'll leave that to you, Sawyer and Lucy. And possibly something with red flowers in it? Can you ask the objects about that, Constance?"

Go on to the next page.

Constance nods. "I can also get us in."

"Right, yes, good," Elwyn says. "After those things are retrieved, Jack, we need you to get the spare key from Mr. Fitzherbert, then hide nearby until the Headmistress returns. Then, lock her in."

"Easy," Jack responds.

Elwyn nods in response. "Sal, can you climb to the top of the school and get a bird's-eye view of things? See if you spot anything suspicious, then report back?"

"No problem."

"Saelor, after Jack locks the Headmistress in, for extra assurance, we'd like you to guard the door. If she's too quiet or tries to get out, use cockroaches. She's terrified of cockroaches."

"How do you know?" you ask, forgetting he can't hear you.

But Constance says, "Pearl wants to know how you know that?"

Oh. Wow. She does know what you're saying. "Thanks, Constance," you say. A slight smile crosses her face.

"Ask Jack and Saelor."

Turn to the next page.

Everyone looks to them. "We pranked her once with the cockroaches from the biology lab. She stayed up on the desk an extra half hour until she was sure we'd put them all away."

Everyone laughs.

Then, they split up and you all go your separate ways. You and Elwyn are on phone duty. Your job is to find a phone that works and call the police.

Everything goes off beautifully except the calling the police part.

There isn't a working phone in the entire school, which has got to be some sort of hazard.

Instead, Elwyn sets off flares. Surely someone will see them and alert the authorities.

Finally, with the Headmistress locked in her office, evidence collected, Mr. Fitzherbert mysteriously nowhere to be found, the police arrive at the door.

The Headmistress and Mr. Fitzherbert are arrested.

Wondering how they knew to come to Old Willow School, Elwyn asks, "Was it the flare?"

Go on to the next page.

"What flare?" the officer says. "We received a strange call with only growling, screeching, and meowing on the other end. We were worried a wild animal had somehow gotten in. We did not expect this!"

You glance behind the police officer, and there, next to his cat door, is Benedict.

Of course. Perhaps he's not all evil after all.

Things get back to normal, better than normal, actually, save the fact you're dead. Your friends make you a cushy cozy ghost room where they often visit.

The End

Mazes

You make your way to Elwyn's room.

Tap-tap-tap.

You tap Elwyn's wooden desk. The sensation is like coarse wool against your fingertips.

He's trying to study, and you know he must hear you, but you can't tell if he's ignoring it because he thinks it's something else or because he's scared of what it might be.

You continue tapping. You try to tap his favorite song, but it doesn't translate. But you do have his attention now. He's searching all over his desk trying to see what could be making the noise. You give up on the tapping and instead push the tip of his pencil into the paper so it draws a jagged but pronounced letter "P."

"P-Pearl?" he asks.

Tap-tap-tap.

You hope he gets the message: that your taps mean *Yes, it's me, dork!*

"What? But how?"

You try to scribble the letters g-h-o-s-t, but it's not legible. You change tactics and work on getting him to follow you to the Headmistress's office.

Go on to the next page.

You knock on the wall until you get to the door. Then you push the door open and knock on the wall outside in the hallway.

Tentatively, Elwyn leaves his room. "You . . . you want me to follow you?"

Knock-knock-knock.

"Okay, but you better be Pearl and not a demon."

You laugh, then give another three knocks.

"Great. Experts claim three knocks are a demon's way of mocking the Holy Trinity, so . . ."

"Fine," you laugh. Elwyn and those overly dramatic paranormal podcasts. "Experts my foot." *Knock-knock.*

"Okay, but that's probably what a demon would do too." He laughs under his breath nervously but follows.

Turn to the next page.

When you reach the Headmistress's office, you find the door is open, which means she isn't far. You give a quick two knocks, hoping to imply urgency.

Continuing to use the knocking, you lead Elwyn to the drawer where the dagger is. He opens it and finds the bloody dagger.

"Is this what killed you, Pearl?"

"I think so. Oh yeah, you can't hear me, sorry." *Knock-knock.*

Before you can figure out how to explain that both the Headmistress and Mr. Fitzherbert are probably in on it, Elwyn rushes across the hall to the sniveling assistant's closet turned office and shouts, "I found this bloody dagger in the Headmistress's office. She killed Pearl! She killed Pearl!"

"Elwyn, no!" you shout.

"Oh my," Mr. Fitzherbert says. His speech is drawn out as if he's considering what to do next. But instead of doing something clever, he simply grabs Elwyn.

You jump and sort of also float high enough to reach one of the trophies he keeps on his shelf and knock it off, so it lands on his head. Mr. Fitzherbert falls to the ground, knocked out cold.

Elwyn and you take off running.

You make your way through the school and escape out the side doors. But as soon as your foot crosses over the boundary of the school and hits the manicured grass, you are picked up into the air. You scream for help, but Elwyn can't hear you. In a flash—so fast you barely register traveling such a distance—you are whisked to the middle of the maze.

Thankfully, Elwyn eventually realizes you're no longer with him and he knows exactly where to look. Well, it's the third place he looks, but he does find you.

You are able to continue communicating at the gazebo by using your knocking and tapping method.

After you've shared everything you know through yes and no questions and knocks on the bench, Elwyn sneaks off the school grounds and alerts the authorities of your death and the Headmistress's and Mr. Fitzherbert's suspicious activities.

Turn to page 178.

178

An investigation finds them guilty of your murder. But they manage to escape during the night and are never caught.

You are stuck in the maze. Every time you try to make your way out, you're returned to the middle.

It's torture.

Elwyn visits every day and tries to time travel you out of there. So far, though, you've only managed to either go too far back in time to when the school was a prison for wayward children, or too far into the future to when the school no longer stands.

Neither scenario is comforting.

The End

Sweet Nothings

You make your way to the kitchen. You knock an entire canister of sugar over and it spills like a cascade of fine sand onto the large butcher block.

Using your finger, you write in the sugar: "Headmistress did it. Dagger in office drawer. Blood."

It's taken you quite some time, but you manage it and it's actually legible.

Miss Loveland finds the note and calls the police. She assumes a student who knew something and was too afraid to tell anyone left the message.

Unfortunately, the message is erased by the time the police arrive.

The police go ahead and do a check based on Miss Loveland's call.

But when they search the Headmistress's drawer, the dagger is mysteriously no longer there.

Stranger still, the Headmistress has sold the school to a seafood restaurateur.

Not only are you stuck as a ghost, but your friends all move away and you have to stare at a lobster tank and smell fish frying for eternity.

The End

Lemmings

It's never too difficult to track Jack and Saelor down. While there are many nooks and crannies in the large school, there are only so many that Jack and Saelor frequent to either play banned betting games or concoct elaborate pranks.

You and Constance stumble upon Old Willow's two most notorious miscreants in what is affectionately referred to as Mrs. Willow's snuggery. It's a room in one of the back turrets where it is rumored the original Headmistress of the home, Mrs. Willow, took her respites. Books and old art materials still line the shelves, and the small space is filled with sitting pillows and two cushy chairs.

You and Constance sneak up on Jack and Saelor who are none the wiser, deeply engrossed in a game of cards.

Constance whispers something under her breath and the two chairs quickly scoot right up behind Jack and Saelor.

Simultaneously, the two of them glance up and see Constance. But before they can react and run, the chairs scoop them up, then tip them back so they can't escape. Constance tosses two lengths of rope toward the chairs. Midair the rope untangles and wraps itself around Jack and Saelor.

You're stunned.

"You've been practicing," you say to Constance.

"No, I've just not been as mean as I could have been to you." She glances over and gives a satisfied grin.

You and Constance work to interrogate Saelor and Jack.

"What do you know about my death?" you say, and Constance repeats your question.

"The plan was for Pearl to be chased into the library by a colony of stinging wasps," Saelor admits, Jack nodding in agreement.

Go on to the next page.

"It sounds bad now, considering . . . but it would have been harmless, really!" Saelor continues.

Jack fights the rope. "I was mad at Pearl for blowing me off last week to hang out with Elwyn in the hedge maze when she had promised to do a past-life regression with me."

You step closer, forgetting Jack can't see you. "What? I never promised!" The nerve.

"We didn't even go through with the prank! We couldn't find her anywhere." Saelor tries to shrug but the restraints hold her back.

"You can let them go," you say to Constance and her inanimate cronies who clearly have questionable morals.

Instantly, the ropes drop, freeing Saelor and Jack.

You and Constance recruit Saelor and Jack, and one by one you interrogate other students into confessing what they know.

Which isn't much. No one is guilty. No one knows or saw anything.

Clearly, someone is lying. You're dead. Whether it was an accident or purposeful, it didn't just magically happen. A dagger did not simply fall from the ceiling.

Not on its own, anyway.

And there's also the many adults who live and work at the school. One student's story stands out to you, and it does involve an adult.

Turn to the next page.

182

Charlie Gene Jenkins is a second-year student who has had many run-ins with trouble and has spent his fair share of time in the Headmistress's office for punishment. His abilities include levitation of himself and objects. He's also an insufferable show-off, and the nephew of the school's cook.

Charlie claims he was in the kitchen helping his aunt prepare muffins for breakfast until midnight the night you died.

"You're not supposed to be out of bed past lights out," you tell him during interrogation. Constance passes your message along.

"I know, but my aunt lets me. Sometimes I can't sleep," he confesses. He goes on to explain he was chopping the carrots for Cook's carrot cake muffins, but that when he went to choose a knife, one of the options was clearly not a chopping knife but a throwing dagger.

"I asked my aunt about it, and she just shrugged, said strange items turn up all the time in her kitchen. She asked me to return it before I went to bed."

"And . . . ?" you prod through Constance.

"And I did." His cheeks flush. Constance orders the chair he sits in to push itself farther into the corner. "Fine! I know I'm not supposed to, but I used my abilities. I was going to levitate the knife back to the common room for Sawyer. But as I was cutting through the library, I think it got stuck somewhere. Maybe on a shelf or in a wall. I panicked and went to bed."

Go on to the next page.

You and the others decide Charlie's story is highly suspicious.

It's no secret he's jealous of Sawyer and that Charlie is his aunt's darling boy. You, Jack, Saelor, and Constance conclude that Cook and Charlie framed Sawyer for your death.

The authorities are called in and Cook and Charlie are taken away for your murder.

That night, as you celebrate with your friends, you all discover a note left in the common room. It's stabbed into the wall with a throwing dagger.

You framed the wrong people. I killed Pearl Maribel. Try to guess who's next?

The End

The Séance

Constance sends out word to the other students. That night, there is a circle of candles.

Several students sneak out of their beds to attend Constance's séance. She doesn't lie. She claims to be trying to reach out to your spirit (and other students whose lives ended here at Old Willow).

Boy does it draw a crowd.

"Take one another's hands. Our connection strengthens the protective circle," Constance says like she's leading a meditation session at the spa your mother visits weekly.

"The ash of the dead connects us to the other realm." Constance walks the circle, dabbing each student's forehead with the ash of something or *someone*. Several students flinch at the thought.

Constance takes her seat in the circle. "Circle of friends, connected by light, protected with the salt of the earth, we request that any spirit willing come forth, join our circle!"

You step over the salt and stand in the middle.

Your plan is to do what you now deem your party tricks—blow out candles, brush the salt from the circle aside, tug on clothes and hair, break something.

"Pearl Margaret Maribel, if you are here, please step forward, show yourself!"

You try to float and slowly lift off the ground. But whereas you've only ever come up a few inches, you are now thrust at least five feet over the circle.

"Whoa! Constance? Did . . . did you do that?"

But she doesn't answer. It's almost like she's in a trance—eyes closed but lids flickering, mumbling something you aren't able to make out.

"Show yourself!" Constance repeats.

Several candles go out and the students collectively gasp.

All eyes are on you.

What the creeps?

Turn to the next page.

Glancing down at your body, you see you're glowing. "Can anyone see me?" you say.

They only stare, jaws agape, eyes wide and fixed. Are they in a trance too?

This goes on as if you are flickering in and out of their vision. They seem to ask you questions, but you can't hear them, and it seems they can't hear you.

You try to force your way out of the circle, but you only succeed in knocking over candles, spreading salt around, and making the curtains at a nearby window wave. You're frozen in this one spot.

Several students get so scared they run away.

Others leave the circle and gather in the corners of the common room.

Constance ends the séance by saying, "This circle is closed, all who entered must go in peace."

And you go, all right.

But where you land is a strange, barren, destitute version of the Old Willow Boarding School. No one lives there. It's empty with overgrown plants and debris winding through it. Half broken down; turrets caved in.

You are officially not a fan of séances.

The End

ABOUT THE ARTISTS

Illustrator: Gabhor Utomo was born in Indonesia. He moved to California to pursue his passion in art. He received his degree from Academy of Art University in San Francisco in spring 2003. Since graduation, he's worked as a freelance illustrator and has illustrated a number of children's books. Gabhor lives with his wife, Dina, and his twin girls in Portland, Oregon.

Cover Artist: Brian Anderson is the author of several children's books, including *The Conjurers Trilogy* as well as the picture books *Nighty Night, Sleepy Sleeps*; *The Prince's New Pet*; and *Monster Chefs*. He is also an optioned screenwriter and the creator of the syndicated comic strip *Dog Eat Doug*, which enjoys an international fan base both online and offline. He lives in North Carolina with his family, which includes a herd of rescued dogs and cats.

Visit www.brianandersonwriter.com for free books!
⊙ *@dogeatdougcomics*

ABOUT THE AUTHOR

Jessika Fleck is a writer, voracious coffee drinker, and knitter—she sincerely hopes to one day discover a way to do all three at once. Until then, she continues failing to resurrect house plants, training to be an archivist, and slowly evolving into a genuine "cat lady." She writes both young adult and middle grade fiction, but has an extra squishy soft spot in her heart for Choose Your Own Adventure. As a child, she and her little brother read Choose Your Own Adventure books nightly and would take turns making the choices. What he still doesn't know is that she would secretly go back on her own and make the opposite choices later! She's thrilled for the opportunity to write the choices this time.

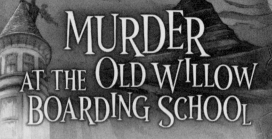

MURDER
AT THE OLD WILLOW
BOARDING SCHOOL

This book is different from other books.

You and YOU ALONE are in charge of what happens in this story.

There are dangers, choices, adventures, and consequences. YOU must use all of your numerous talents and much of your enormous intelligence. The wrong decision could end in disaster—even death. But don't despair. At any time, YOU can go back and make another choice, alter the path of your story, and change its result.

YOU are a student named Pearl at the Old Willow Boarding School for Gifted Children. After waking up from a strange dream, you go to breakfast with your friends and feel oddly alone. No one looks at you and no one is answering your questions. It's not until you hear a scream and rush to the library to find the sight of your lifeless body that you realize YOU ARE DEAD. Now, as a ghost, you need to solve the mystery of your own murder—but who can you trust? And can you figure out who is behind this crime before the killer strikes again?